M000015185

SPELLS & SHELVES

A LIBRARY WITCH MYSTERY

ELLE ADAMS

This book was written, produced and edited in the UK, where some spelling, grammar and word usage will vary from US English.

Copyright © 2019 Elle Adams
All rights reserved.

To be notified when Elle Adams's next book is released, sign up to her author newsletter.

"**A**urora!" shouted my boss.

I closed the book I'd been reading under the desk. No customers had shown up all afternoon, but Abe hated me reading on the job, even though books surrounded me on every side and the shelves were positively overflowing. Who could resist the temptation? Besides, business wasn't exactly booming.

"Yes?" I called back.

"I'm going into the storeroom," he said. "Please watch the desk, and if I catch you reading, I'll be extremely displeased."

"Wouldn't dream of it," I responded. Reading in a bookshop? Perish the thought.

I fidgeted, smoothing out the wrinkles in my skirt. Abe liked me to show up dressed respectably, which meant plain, drab coloured skirts past my knees, neat shirts and cardigans, and my hair pulled back in a bun that made me look decades older than my twenty-five years. It fitted the place's solemn atmosphere, but considering every other shop was bursting with glittery Christmas decorations, it was no wonder everyone overlooked our gloomy little establishment. Besides, I knew for a fact that Dad used to come to work in jeans and a T-shirt all the time. When he was around, I wouldn't have called the place gloomy or solemn, either. But that was then.

I sneaked a look over my shoulder, made sure Abe was out of sight, then opened the book again. *Honestly.* Resisting the temptation was like avoiding looking at a box of chocolates directly in front of me. Nobody was out book shopping on a dismal winter day like today. The Christmas shoppers all went to the big department stores in the nearby cities, not second-hand bookshops tucked into a corner off the high street of a small village in the middle of nowhere.

I had no reason to complain. I loved working with books. I didn't have to make small talk with customers or push sales initiatives in their faces or deal with complaints. Admittedly, having complaints would require having customers. I dusted shelves every day, set up displays to look welcoming and interesting, and put up with Abe's grumbling about my rearranging things, but each year brought fewer visitors.

Abe had offered me the assistant job after Dad's death in a car accident, since he'd left his entire share of the shop to his former business partner. Even after three years, Abe still paid me a shade above minimum wage. Laney kept saying he was exploiting me, and maybe it was true, but I owed it to Dad to keep the place running. The shop had been his whole life.

"Aurora?" Abe called. "You're not reading, are you?"

"Nope." I closed the book again.

Abe was the only person who called me by my full name. I went by Rory to everyone else, but the boss kept a professional veneer even though he and my dad had been best friends and we'd known one another for most of my life. He and Dad might have been work partners, but they couldn't be more different personality-wise. We'd already had two arguments this week about Dad's old journal. Abe had found it in the back room and I'd caught him tossing it in the bin. I'd protested, and he'd thrown up his hands and said fine, I was welcome to any of Dad's old junk. I'd fished it out of the bin and opened it, expecting to find an account of my dad's courtship with Mum or even his years running the bookshop. Instead, I'd found a bunch of gibberish.

Not only was the book written in a text I couldn't read, it didn't match up with any language I could find either—and I'd searched the entire bookshop for possible matches until Abe had informed me the whole thing was made-up. Writing a book in code and then losing the translator document was such a Dad thing to do, but it made the journal worthless, according to Abe. I still carried it everywhere with me, on the off-chance that I found the solution to the code stashed on a shelf somewhere.

I'd been coming into the shop since before I could read. Most of my childhood memories involved toddler-me waddling among the shelves, kid-me burying her face in a book for hours to escape the outside world after Mum died of cancer, and teen-me seeking solace in a corner where none of the school bullies could bother me. Now, adult-me sat here in the same spot I'd occupied for three years, contemplating yet another reread of the shop's paltry collection of fantasy novels. Most of them were old coming-of-age tales of farm boys embarking on grand adventures and saving the world. My birthday had brought nothing of the kind. Then again, no twenty-five-year-old bookshop assistants got Hogwarts letters or mysterious prophecies or grand destinies. Shame, because most adults I knew were in dire need of a little magic in their lives. Abe being a prime example.

The door flew open. I jumped in my seat, startled. Normally a little bell rang when someone entered, but the three people who glided into the shop made no sound at all.

3

If I hadn't been looking at the door at that precise moment, I'd never have heard them enter.

One of them approached the counter. He had slick dark hair and a face as pale as a piece of carved white stone. Not a typical customer. He looked like one of the wax statues at Madame Tussauds had come to life and walked into the shop.

"Can I help you?" For some reason, I had the impulse to check my bag under the desk to make sure Dad's journal was still there.

"I highly doubt you can," he said, in a posh accent. Not only did he dress like he'd stepped out of a Victorian novel, he also talked like it.

As for his two companions—they were suddenly right behind him. How had they moved that fast? I definitely needed a break. I'd been working long shifts for so long I'd lost track of the days. No wonder my attention span was a little rusty.

"Were you looking for a book?" I asked, since he didn't seem inclined to break the silence. "We have a large selection of—"

He smiled. His teeth were perfectly even and blindingly white. For a moment, his face blurred, showing me pointed canines. Then in another blink, he looked normal.

Normal? Nothing about these three men was normal. The other two moved closer, crowding my desk. Boxing me in.

I sat completely still. I should call Abe, but my throat was dry, and my mouth felt too numb to open. My sweaty fingers dug into the sides of my wooden chair.

"Yes," said the man. "I was looking for a book. It belonged to a man named Roger Hawthorn."

Dad. Had Dad known these men? "That's my father," I managed to say. "He died three years ago."

"My condolences," said the man. "Yes, I know he died. I'm looking for his journal."

My heart missed a beat. "Excuse me?"

"Did you mishear?" He enunciated each word. "I'm looking for the journal that belonged to Roger Hawthorn."

The journal's weight in my rucksack pressed into my leg. I might not be able to read it, but I did not want to give it to him.

"Sorry, I don't have it," I lied. "We only sell books, not journals."

"You're lying," he said, his words precise, certain. As though he'd looked into my mind and plucked my thoughts right out. Sweat gathered on the back of my neck, and my legs itched to run. I'd just celebrated my birthday, and I wanted to survive to see my next.

I opened my mouth to call Abe, and he shook his head, almost imperceptibly. "If you call your supervisor, Aurora, he won't come. Trust me, it'll be much easier if you hand me the book."

I rested a trembling hand on the desk, my fingers snagging the book I'd left out on display, titled *The Beginner's Guide to Horticulture.* It'd been there for years and nobody had ever bought it.

The waxwork man's gaze dropped to my hand on the book and he took a step back. *Fast.* This time I couldn't blame my tired eyes—he'd moved faster than any human being had the right to.

"Are you sure you won't be persuaded to give up the journal?" he asked.

My hand remained clenched on the book. Something in his expression shifted. He raised a hand and I froze, but all he did was scatter a handful of something on the desk. It looked like… sand.

"You'll regret your decision," said the man, as calm and

5

matter-of-fact as though we were chatting at the supermarket. "Remember my name. It's Mortimer Vale."

And in a blink, the three men were gone. Only the sound of the door closing behind them showed they'd been here at all.

You're officially cracking up, Rory.

I stared at the fragments of sand scattered on the desk for an instant. Then I got up, grabbed the wastepaper basket, and used a piece of paper to brush the sand into it. Bits of sand clung to the paper. From this angle, they looked orange-red. Kind of like—

Fire.

The paper was on fire. So was the wastepaper basket. I dropped both with a cry of alarm, and the flames leapt perilously close to the desk.

"Aurora?" came Abe's muffled voice from the back room.

This can't be happening. Paper didn't spontaneously burst into flames. I looked wildly around for a fire extinguisher. What had Abe done with it? We didn't even have a working fire alarm.

An image filled my head, of the ornate bookshelves engulfed in flames. Of Dad's legacy burning to the ground.

No. I backed up into the desk, knocking over the *Beginner's Guide to Horticulture*. A pen rolled off the desk and I caught in on instinct, and a weird tingling sensation ran up my arm. At the same time, the *Beginner's Guide to Horticulture* began to glow, its pages turning gold. *Please tell me that's not about to catch on fire, too.*

A second shiver went up my arm, stronger than the last one. I froze, gripped by an uncontrollable urge to scream—no, write. The pen moved in my hand, scratching out my last desperate thought onto the open page of the record book —*Stop!*

The fire in the wastepaper basket went out, the flames

vanishing from existence. I stared, stupefied. I couldn't have done that. Scribbling the word *stop* on a page didn't make fires go out.

Right?

I stood stock-still. The *Beginner's Guide to Horticulture* was no longer glowing, the tingling in my arm had disappeared, and the lingering smell of flames from the wastepaper basket was the only reminder that it'd been on fire at all.

I jumped when the door at the back of the shop opened and Abe walked in. "What happened here, Aurora?" he asked. "What's that smell?"

"A fire," I gasped. "That paper—it caught fire. By itself. But it's okay, the fire went out."

His steps halted. "Caught fire? Were you playing with matches?"

"What? No."

He strode over to the bin, peering into it. "Did you think you could smoke in this shop?"

"No," I said. "Three men, strangers, they came into the shop." If I said 'I think they used magical sand to set the bin on fire', he'd think I was bonkers. "They used a lighter," I lied. "On the paper in the bin."

"Three men?" He dropped the bin and marched over to the door, yanking it open. A cold blast of winter air rushed in, but nobody was outside. As I'd expected, the men had vanished, leaving no trace behind.

I swallowed as Abe let the door swing shut, his face stern, demanding an explanation.

"As I said, the fire went out. No harm done." I didn't sound convincing. My hands shook with tremors, while the word *stop* stood out on the page behind me like a brand. I felt lightheaded, too, as though I was about to faint.

He shook his head. "Aurora, there's nobody outside."

"They left a… minute ago." And they'd moved impossibly fast. "I don't smoke. And I'd never risk damaging the books."

He paced back to the desk, eyeing the word *stop* on the record book's open page. "Did you write this?"

I opened and closed my mouth. Abe knew my handwriting. There was no use feigning ignorance. "I…"

He ripped the page out of the record book. I flinched at the noise. "Aurora, I've made a lot of allowances for you. But this—" He threw the paper into the bin—"it won't do at all."

"I didn't do anything," I said. "The men who came in said they were looking for Dad's journal."

His brows shot up. "Journal?"

"The one he gave me," I said. "I don't know why they wanted it."

Abe shook his head vigorously. "Aurora, you've been working too many long hours. Nobody was here."

"But the first man said he knew Dad—"

"Aurora." The word was sharp. Cutting. "You're clearly in no fit state to work today."

My throat closed up. "It's the truth."

"Aurora, take a seat."

That did not sound promising.

I walked behind the desk and sank into the chair. Dad's journal bumped against my legs in my rucksack. I'd never have given it up to the strangers, but how could I convince Abe I wasn't lying when every moment that passed made me less certain that I hadn't hallucinated the whole thing?

"Aurora, the last three years have been difficult for both of us." Abe gave a pause, and I dipped my head in acknowledgement. "Since your father's death… I admit, I didn't expect him to leave the shop entirely to me. And I understand why you felt the need to take his place. But the truth is, I can barely afford to keep an assistant. And when you do things that damage our reputation…"

My heart beat so fast it nearly escaped my chest. I blinked repeatedly, and a glow caught my eye. The *Beginner's Guide to Horticulture's* pages shone, their white pages glowing golden from within.

I pointed at the book. "Do you see that?"

His gaze jumped to the book, then back to me. "What is it this time?"

"Do you not see it? It's... glowing." I trailed off. The glow was already dying down. Maybe I really was losing my mind.

Abe shook his head. "The truth is, your father would want you to strike out on your own," he said. "He wouldn't have wanted you to stay here forever."

But I want to.

He tried a smile which was more of a grimace. "I really think it's for the best that I let you go."

"Please," I said. "I don't—"

"We'll discuss it tomorrow," he said. "Go home, Aurora."

Dismissed. No—fired. *Fired.* Like those flames, which had vanished into nothingness.

Who set fire to a bookshop? What kind of sick monster would do that? I'd never seen the waxwork-looking man before in my life, but he'd spoken like we knew one another or were in on a shared secret. And now, thanks to him, I'd lost my job.

Abe watched as I retrieved my rucksack, checking Dad's journal was still there. What was so important that those men had felt the need to threaten me over it? I couldn't even read it. Nobody could.

The bitter air wrapped around me as I left the shop, cutting through my thick cardigan. I shivered, hoisting my rucksack higher on my shoulders. I was jobless. How would I pay rent? Employers in a small town like this one didn't care about my MA. I'd have to get a minimum wage job, in which case, I could say goodbye to my flat. I'd barely been able to pay the deposit as it was. Most of my friends had moved to Leeds or Manchester or Birmingham. Big cities with job opportunities. I'd only stayed here because of the shop, and now I'd lost it.

Tears froze on my cheeks. I wiped them away, reaching in my pocket for my keys—then stopped dead.

Three men stood outside my apartment block, looking up at the third floor. Specifically, at my window. It was the same men who'd been in the shop. I knew from their heights and the eerie way they stood. Absolutely still, like they were statues fused to the pavement.

Who *were* they? And how had they known where I lived?

I looked around. Nobody else walked around the high street on a freezing Wednesday afternoon in December. They were inside in the warmth or at work.

I backed up a few steps, and my phone started to buzz with an incoming call.

The first waxwork man turned in my direction. "Ah, Aurora," he said. "I thought you might have reconsidered your decision."

"Get away from my flat." My voice sounded high, scared, and I cast a desperate look at the windows of the other flats in the hope that someone might look outside. Nobody did.

The man—Mortimer Vale, he'd said his name was—smiled. "Just give us what we need. Give me the journal."

"I don't have it."

The journal's weight in my rucksack pressed against my spine. Maybe if I threw it at them, it'd buy me enough time to run and call the police. But something in me rebelled at the idea, and besides, they'd easily catch me if they moved as fast as they'd done in the shop. My phone was still ringing, its traitorous buzz giving me away.

"Then I'll have to take it by force."

The man moved. I turned and ran, grabbing my phone as

I did so. To call the police, not whoever's epically bad timing had sent three loonies on my tail. What had I ever done to tick them off? I was just a bookshop assistant. No, ex-bookshop assistant. I'd never done anything illegal or odd in my life.

Except stop fires with my bare hands?

The phone's buzzing ceased, and a female voice said, "Hello, is this Aurora Hawthorn?"

"Sorry, I'm in the middle of an emergency," I gasped out. "Can I call you back?"

"I'd keep running," said the female speaker on the other end.

"Excuse me?"

"Keep running," she repeated. "Towards the river or the nearest source of running water you can find."

I looked up. The river was across the road from me. How did the caller know where I was? I shoved my phone in my pocket and picked up the pace, flat-out sprinting.

"I wouldn't run that way." The voice came from my pocket. Her voice was so loud, it was like she was standing right next to me. "Go to the water. Before they catch you."

"Who are you? Why are you watching me?" My breath came out in pants. My footsteps hammered on the road, and when I risked a glance behind me, the man was close enough to catch my eye and smile.

They could catch me in a heartbeat, but they were toying with me.

"Keep moving," said the voice on the other end. "You're almost there."

I veered to the right, towards the bridge. There were no cars around—and in a blink, the man appeared in front of me, blocking my path.

I gasped, skidding to a halt.

The woman's voice rang out from my pocket. "Don't panic, love. Get into the water."

There was a path down to the bank, but it was a drop a couple of metres off the ground. The other two men were closing in behind me. Nowhere to run.

"They're vampires, love. They can't cross running water. If you get in, they won't be able to touch you."

"I—what?"

Total strangers calling me 'love' and talking about vampires was the last thing I needed when my life was in dire peril. I gave a last desperate look at the nearby road. Nobody was coming to my rescue. I had nothing to lose.

I jumped off the bank, my feet hitting the shallows. If nothing else, they might hesitate to follow me into the water. Or maybe they'd drown me. They'd already tried to set me on fire today, after all.

I waded into the water, my feet dragging, the two strangers watching from the bank. They looked angry—and they weren't following. I glanced at the bridge and saw the third man eyeing me with his lip curled. He didn't move to follow me, either.

"Are you in the water?" the woman's voice came from my pocket.

"Yes."

"Good. Stay there. This isn't the best place to explain, but you're probably feeling very confused right now."

You think? "That's one way of putting it."

"Got the sharp tongue from your father, I see." The woman chuckled.

"Look—who are you?" I asked. "I'm standing ankle-deep in water with three madmen who tried to burn down my place of employment staring creepily at me."

"I'll come and deal with them once Candace gets here.

The short answer, love, is that you're a witch. And I'm Adelaide, your aunt."

"You—*what?*"

A shout of triumph came from the other end of the line. "I knew I put that transporter spell somewhere."

"Ready?" said another female voice in the background. "Estelle, are you coming?"

"I wouldn't miss it."

The call cut out. The next thing I knew, there was someone else standing in the water behind me. I jumped, tripped over a rock, and sank into deeper water to my waist. Holding my phone out of reach of the water, I righted my balance, staring at the odd woman behind me. She wore what appeared to be a long black cloak, which billowed around her in the murky water.

"Cold, isn't it?" The woman, whose voice matched the one I'd heard on the phone, waded forwards a few steps. "It's a pleasure to meet you in person."

She was tall and curvy with thick dark red hair bouncing to her shoulders in waves. Pale skin. Freckles. Like me.

Like Dad.

"You're in trouble, aren't you?" she said gently.

I must be dreaming. I waved helplessly at the vampires— no, they were *not* vampires—and said, "They tried to break into my flat."

"I know, dear," she said. "Don't worry, Candace is on her way."

"Who's Candace?"

With a popping noise, two more women appeared on either side of the men by the water. There was a flash of fiery light and I cringed back, remembering the burning shelves and the close call I'd had.

The two men fled, their figures blurring as they disappeared from sight. The third, still on the bridge, moved his gaze to me. His eyes narrowed.

"Leave," said the woman in the water behind me. "If you come anywhere near my family again, I will see to it that you regret it for the rest of your existence."

Without a word, the third man vanished, leaving nothing but the bare concrete bridge behind.

I was saved. I wanted to lie down. Problem: I was still waist-deep in the river, surrounded by strangers who claimed to be my relations.

The woman in the water said, "Don't just stand there shivering. Come with me. I'll get you out of this place."

I didn't move. "Who are you? What in the world is going on?"

"I told you, I'm your Aunt Adelaide," she said. "That's Candace and Estelle. And you're Aurora. I've heard all about you."

I shivered. If not for the icy water drenching me to the waist, I'd be certain I was dreaming. None of this made sense.

"Don't worry," said the woman she'd called Candace. "I gave them a good scare. They won't bother you again, especially when you come to the library."

I frowned. "The what?"

Adelaide waded to the shore. "The library, of course," she said. "Your new home."

2

M y heart missed a beat. "I'm sorry, what?"

"We should have this conversation some-where more appropriate," she said, climbing out of the river onto the bank, her cloak dragging with the weight of the water. I stood shivering instead of following. She couldn't be my aunt. I didn't have any family left. Abe was the closest to a living relative I had, and now…

Adelaide waved an impatient hand. "Come on, climb out. The last thing we need is the normals to spot us. I'd prefer not to have to doctor any memories."

She was speaking English, but the words refused to connect in my brain. Vampires or not, though, the men had taken off. And I needed to get home, dry off, and lose myself in a good book until reality made sense again.

"You'll catch your death of cold like that," she said, and pulled out a stick of wood. "Come on, get out of the water."

Something in her voice told me she was used to giving orders to people. Besides, mad or not, standing in the river to prove a point wasn't a smart idea.

Pointing the stick at her cloak, she gave it a flick. In an

instant, the cloak was dry and completely clean as though she'd never set foot in the river.

I got out of the water, climbing up the filthy bank. Adelaide waved the stick again, and the water vanished from my clothes. My sopping wet cardigan stopped weighing me down, and the cold air no longer bit through my sodden clothes. But the shivering didn't stop. Unless my brain had conjured up a detailed illusion, she'd waved a magic wand and used a spell on me.

Aunt—*not* my Aunt—Adelaide watched me closely, as though to gauge my reaction.

"Who are you?" I asked. "You can't be my aunt. I'd have met you before."

"Complicated rules, dear. Why not take us to your home? It'll be much more comfortable. I have a feeling we'll need to chat for a while."

I opened my mouth to protest and then closed it. My little flat wasn't designed for entertaining visitors. It barely had room for me to live in it. On the other hand, whoever these women were, they'd saved my life. The least I could do was offer them a cup of tea, Dad-style, and ask them for a reasonable explanation for today's events.

I retraced my steps home, Adelaide at my side. The other two women walked close behind. All three of them wore the same clothes, long silver-lined black cloaks that looked downright impractical to chase vampires around in. Yet they acted like they did this every day.

I slowed as I reached my flat, pulling out my keys. The apartment block was modern with a decent security system, but if the vampires had wanted to get inside, I had the distinct impression security codes wouldn't have got in the way. Keys in hand, I hesitated on the threshold.

"They won't be inside, love," said Adelaide. "Vampires can't enter without an invitation."

I walked into the entryway, then turned to face the three people who claimed to be my relatives. "Okay," I said. "Say I believe the whole vampire thing... they came into the book-shop without being invited."

Adelaide waved a hand. "Shops and public places are different. Which floor do you live on?"

"Third, but the elevator isn't working."

"No problem." The younger witch, the one she'd called Estelle, pulled out a stick of wood and pointed it at the closed metal doors of the lift. There was a popping sound, and the doors sprang open.

Okay...

The three women crowded into the lift, and I joined them before the doors closed. The mirrored walls showed all four of us crammed together. Adelaide was either a relation or a ridiculously good lookalike because her eyes and freckles were Dad's—and mine. Candace, the second aunt, was tall and willowy, like me, her auburn hair wild and loose. And the younger woman, Estelle, had a similar figure to Adelaide and her hair cut to chin-length. She smiled at me in the mirror. She had Dad's eyes, too.

I was thoroughly unnerved by the time I stepped out of the lift onto the tattered carpet of the third-floor corridor and unlocked the door to my flat.

"This is... cosy," Adelaide commented.

My face heated as the three newcomers looked curiously around the cramped space of my one-room studio flat. I didn't think it was that untidy—all the books were neatly arranged on the shelves, there weren't any clothes lying on the floor and I kept the kitchen clean—but I detected a hint of pity in Adelaide's expression that suggested she'd expected something akin to a penthouse apartment.

"Uh..." I pulled out the chair at the tiny desk in the

corner. "I don't have enough chairs. I don't often have visitors over."

Now I sounded pathetic. While I might spend a lot of time reading, I liked people just fine—I just liked books better. But Laney was the only person who came over on a frequent basis. Social butterfly, I was not.

"Not a problem." Estelle waved her wand, and a sofa popped into existence, followed by two armchairs.

I stared for a moment, then rested my hand on the top of the sofa. It was solid. Solid enough to pass out on, anyway.

"I fetched them from the library, don't worry." Estelle nodded to Adelaide. "Where do you want to start?"

"Make some tea," said Adelaide. "Aurora looks like she needs it."

I smiled weakly and collapsed into an armchair.

"Is she going to faint?" Candace squinted at me. "Put your head between your legs. Or is it behind your ears? I never remember."

"I'll make the tea," said Estelle, bounding over to the kitchen. "It'll make you feel better."

"Yes, it will." Adelaide stepped to my side. "Candace, stop staring at her. You're not helping."

Candace tutted and took the other armchair. "If it's any consolation, dearie, this is about to become the best day of your life."

I had my sincere doubts. I rested my head on my knees, my considerably crinkled skirt bunching around my ankles.

I was officially at rock bottom. I had no job. By the month's end, I'd lose my home. As for my family... it made no sense that Dad wouldn't have told me if I had a whole pack of relatives who somehow knew there were strange men after his journal. Oh, and who could appear out of thin air. And do magic.

It made even less sense that a bunch of strangers would

be chasing me *or* Dad, come to that. Why did they want his journal so much?

I looked up when Estelle reappeared, wielding a tray. She'd made tea and scraped together some biscuits on a plate. I'd forgotten I had any. Maybe she'd conjured them with that wand of hers.

Wands. Right. I'd deal with *that* later. First, I turned to the woman still gawking at me from the neighbouring armchair.

"So you're my aunt, too?" I asked. I'd get the *newfound family* part out the way first.

"Yes, I'm your aunt Candace," she said, stuffing half a biscuit in her mouth. "Rescue missions are hungry work."

Adelaide rolled her eyes and took a seat on the sofa. "Don't mind her. We haven't seen so much excitement in weeks."

"Oh." I paused, trying to get my thoughts together. "You're my dad's sisters. He never mentioned you before. And..." I turned to the third newcomer, who offered me the tray. I took a mug—one of my only nice ones—and she sat in the remaining seat on the sofa.

"I'm Estelle, your cousin," said the younger woman. "Your Aunt Adelaide is my mother."

"Cousin," I repeated. "I have two aunts and a cousin who Dad forgot to mention for my entire life?"

"Two cousins," said Estelle. "Cass is busy running the library while we're gone. Three vampires are too much for one person to deal with."

One vampire was too much for me. My hand gripped the mug tightly.

"Drink that, dear," Aunt Adelaide said. "It'll make you feel better."

The tea smelled odd, herbal. I wasn't normally a fan of flavoured tea, but a warm drink sounded like heaven right now. A warm drink and a good book.

I took a long sip. Warmth spread through my body all the way to my toes, and my racing heart slowed. I no longer felt like I might faint. My head cleared enough to present a dozen new questions.

"You had my number, Aunt Adelaide," I said. "How? And how did you know I was in danger?"

"Oh, I set up a spell to watch you," Aunt Adelaide said. "When Roger died, I decided to keep an eye on you in case you were ever in trouble. I left one of our books in the shop, with a spell on it so nobody could buy it. It was on the front display."

"Was it called *The Beginner's Guide to Horticulture*, by any chance?" I asked. The book had glowed when the vampires showed up, and again when Abe was firing me.

"Yes, it was," said Aunt Adelaide. "We did it at the funeral. I'm sorry we weren't able to show our faces, but there are rules, and we didn't know if you were magical or not."

My insides pitched down. "You weren't at the funeral. I'd remember if you were."

My aunts Candace and Adelaide exchanged glances.

"We were," Aunt Adelaide said gently. "As I said, there are rules. We can't reveal ourselves to normals. So we set a watch on you to alert us if it turned out you had magic."

"Magic." I slumped back in my seat, clutching the mug to my chest. "Dad was normal. A normal. That's like... Muggles, right?" I couldn't believe I was even having this conversation.

But whether they were lying about being related to Dad or not, I'd seen things today that I couldn't rationally explain away. Vampires who moved swifter than light and started a fire with a sprinkle of sand. Strange women who looked like Dad, who dried my clothes with a wave of a wand. And I'd stopped a fire using... magic.

"Right," Estelle said. "We're not allowed to expose our

magic to normals. No exceptions. That's why we couldn't reveal ourselves at the funeral. We try to keep a low profile."

"Dad didn't tell me a thing." I looked at the floor, confused emotions warring inside me.

"Well, he married a normal, see," said Aunt Adelaide. "The rules are clear: don't tell normals about the magical world. So, he left our world behind and decided to raise you as a normal. But I felt when you used magic, Aurora."

"Rory," I mumbled. "Most people call me Rory. When I stopped the fire—that was magic?"

"Stopped the fire?" Estelle asked.

"The spell didn't show us what you did," Aunt Candace put in. "It warned us you were in danger.

"It was at the bookshop," I said. "I—Dad's bookshop. But those…" I couldn't say 'vampires'. "Those men tried to burn it down. They started a fire."

"And you used magic to put out the fire?" Estelle guessed.

I shook my head. "That book—the one you mentioned—started glowing, and something… weird happened." I grasped for the words to describe the way I'd felt—the sudden urge to grab the pen and write. "I wrote the word *stop*. And it stopped."

"You wrote it?" Estelle's brows shot up.

Aunt Candace leaned forwards eagerly. Aunt Adelaide had frozen with her mug halfway to her mouth.

"Yes…" What had I said wrong? "It was mad. I was in front of a burning bin and my first instinct was to write on the paper. No wonder my boss kicked me out." I laughed hollowly, the calming effects of the tea dissolving into the impulse to curl up and scream into a pillow instead.

"No, you're not mad," Aunt Adelaide said quickly. "I'm just surprised. You've had no training. You're entirely new to the magical world, yet you did genuine biblio-witchery right

21

on the first try. I assumed when you used magic, it was the other sort."

"I... didn't understand a word of that, to be honest." I put the mug down on the table. "What did I do wrong?"

"Nothing," Estelle said. "Nothing at all. You did magic *right*. Few untrained witches could have done it."

My head hurt. 'Look," I said. "Not that I don't appreciate you coming to my rescue, but I lost my job today, and I need to find another one otherwise I won't be able to make next month's rent payment. Maybe we can talk about this another time?"

The two aunts exchanged glances.

"Of course it's your choice," Aunt Adelaide said carefully, setting her mug on the table. "I did wonder, though—what did the vampires want from you?"

"A journal." I reached for my rucksack and unzipped it, removing Dad's small leather-bound book. "I don't understand why they wanted it. I can't even read it. Abe couldn't either. He wrote it in some sort of code that can't be translated."

The three women leaned over the journal. Aunt Candace's hands grabbed for it, but Aunt Adelaide got there first. "Hmm."

I sat stiffly, not liking the journal being out of my hands after the close call I'd had with the vampires.

"It's written in code, all right," Aunt Adelaide said. "Not a typical magical one either. We'll have to look it up."

Aunt Candace's expression suggested Christmas had come early. "Yes, we will. May I take this?"

Estelle stepped in. "It's Aurora's—Rory's. Right?"

I nodded gratefully. "We found it in the back room of the shop. Abe said I should throw it away, but... I never thought anyone would threaten me over it."

"They won't threaten you again," Aunt Adelaide said

confidently. "That said—it'd be much easier if you came with us to the library. No need to worry about your things, we can transport them later."

"Did you say, 'library'?"

"We own the place," Estelle said. "Well, Grandma did, but she died the year I was born."

"Grandma?" I'd had a grandmother who'd died before I'd had the chance to meet her? "Dad never talked about her either. He didn't mention a library."

"The library is special," said Estelle. "You'll like it, I think."

I looked around my sparse, small flat. "I don't know about this. I have a life here." I might not have much, but it was mine.

"Of course you do," said Aunt Candace, a hint of impatience in her voice. "But when vampires are fixated on a goal, they don't give up easily. The moment you leave this building, you'll be at risk. And that's assuming they don't ask one of the other residents to invite them into the apartment block."

My mouth fell open. "They can do that?"

"Vampires are... very clever," said Aunt Candace. Her tone suggested that wasn't necessarily a bad thing.

"You mean dangerous," said Estelle. "Don't worry, Rory— they'll never be able to follow you to the library. It's miles away."

"Miles away?" I echoed. "I don't know—I can't just leave without telling anyone."

Who would I tell, though, aside from Laney? Even she'd have trouble believing it.

"We'll take care of everything," Aunt Adelaide said firmly. "You're family, after all."

Family. I never thought I'd have one again. "Suppose I say yes, and I come with you—wait, where do you live?"

"A coastal town named Ivory Beach," said Estelle. "Paranormals live in isolated communities without normals. It's easier to be ourselves that way. And we own the library, like I said."

"I'm not a... paranormal," I said. "I don't know anything about that world."

"You're definitely paranormal," Aunt Adelaide said. "If you hadn't already used magic to stop that fire, there's a simple test." She held out a pen and a blank notepad.

I took them from her. "What am I supposed to do with this?"

"Pick a spell... I think levitation is a good one. Write the word, *Rise.* And think very hard about that mug." She pointed to the mug I'd put on the table.

It's not like I've got anything to lose at this point. I pressed the nib of the pen to the page, trying to focus on the mug and nothing else.

A tingling sensation rushed up my right arm, from the pen, and an overwhelming urge to write claimed me again. The word *rise* all but rushed out of my pen and I let the notepad fall from my hands.

The mug floated up off the table and hovered in mid-air.

I sat completely still, my hand still tingling. *It's real. It's all real.*

Aunt Adelaide beamed at me. "We have a very particular style of magic, Aurora. We're biblio-witches. We can weave spells from words. Most witches use wands—we do, too, when the occasion calls for it—but our best strength comes from the pen."

I picked the mug out of the air before it fell. "You mean I can write things and they'll come true?"

"Within limits," said Aunt Adelaide. "That was a simple spell, but you clearly have a lot of innate talent."

"I don't know why that's a surprise," Aunt Candace said.

"Of course she's one of us. She worked in a bookshop, for the goddess's sake."

I retrieved the notepad from where I'd dropped it. The word *rise* stared back at me. How could a word hold that kind of power?

I looked up at my aunts. "How did I not know I was magical before?"

"When a paranormal chooses to live among humans, they have to be careful," explained Aunt Candace. "Your father had to swear not to use any magic when humans were watching, for a start. When you were born, he had to choose whether to let you develop the potential for magic or not. If I had to guess, he opted to suppress your powers entirely."

"But if he was magical, then why not use it to save his own life?" I swallowed. "He died when his car went off the road three winters ago. Couldn't he have used a spell to stop it?"

Aunt Adelaide shook her head, sympathy in her eyes. "Magic has its limitations, Rory. I'm sorry."

My stomach sank. "So how is it I turned out to have magic, if my dad stopped it?"

"The spell we put on that book to alert us when you were in danger must have unlocked your own magic, too," said Aunt Adelaide. "These things can happen, on rare occasions."

I put down the pen and paper on the arm of the chair. "Dad went my whole life without telling me a thing."

"He had to," she said gently. "It's the rules."

I was starting to strongly dislike those rules. They'd kept Dad from most of his family for my entire life. "So he left your town and never came back?"

"Oh, we still saw one another," Aunt Adelaide. "Not as often as I'd have liked, though. I wished we could have seen you too, Rory. Your dad had so many positive things to say about you. I have no doubt you'll fit right in at the library."

"Absolutely," Estelle said. "If you want to come with us now, pack your essentials in a suitcase. We can bring the rest over ourselves. The bookshelves can be transported as they are, I think, but let me know if you have any specific requests."

Her words made my head spin. Was I seriously considering running off with my newfound relatives? I'd pick them over the vampires, but Laney would need an explanation and the idea of flinging myself headfirst into the unknown was as terrifying as those flames.

"Sorry, I just got overexcited," Estelle said. "Take your time."

Aunt Candace made a dissatisfied noise. "You do remember you left Cass in charge of managing the front desk, don't you? She's probably started a brawl by now."

"Oh, she'll be fine," said Aunt Adelaide. "If you want to stay here, we can put spells on the place to deter the vampires, but they won't work if you leave your flat."

I pictured those vampires standing outside my door all night and shuddered at the mental image. My aunts were offering me the only way out possible. That was clear.

I got up from the armchair and walked to my wardrobe where I kept my old suitcase. The two aunts turned away and exchanged a murmured conversation I didn't even try to eavesdrop on. I opened my wardrobe instead, finding row after row of drab cardigans and long skirts. A lump grew in my throat.

I grabbed the suitcase first, leaving it open on the floor, then shoved the coat hangers aside and grabbed my old jeans. T-shirts. Casual clothes. Outfit after outfit, I tossed into the suitcase. Then I closed the wardrobe door on my old work clothes, leaving them all behind. I wouldn't need them where I was going. Maybe I'd get one of those black cloaks the others wore.

I can't believe I'm doing this.

I shoved the thought aside and went back to packing. Vampires were hunting me. I was backed into a corner, and yet I had the opportunity of a lifetime.

Ten minutes later, I'd packed all the essentials, and wheeled my suitcase over to the others.

"Is that it?" asked Aunt Adelaide, eyeing my battered rucksack and small suitcase.

My face heated. "It's... well, I don't have much, aside from the books. It's hard to even afford rent on a bookshop assistant's salary."

Almost impossible, actually. When I'd taken the job, I'd been a graduate filled with hopes and ambitions to make the bookshop into something Dad would be proud of. Instead, here I was throwing myself on the mercy of a group of strangers.

Strangers Dad had known.

I swallowed hard. "I'm ready."

Estelle broke into a grin, while Aunt Candace pulled a notebook from her pocket.

"Wrong one," Aunt Adelaide said. "I don't think Rory wants to be part of one of your adventures."

I opened my mouth to ask what she meant, but Aunt Candace switched the first notepad for another and wrote a word on the topmost page.

The next second, we'd vanished.

3

Soft carpet replaced my threadbare rug. Towering shelves filled the space in front of me and on my right. Curved wooden balconies divided one floor from the next. I counted five stories, each filled with endless shelves.

If not for Aunt Adelaide's snapping her fingers, I'd probably have stood there staring all day. In a snap, my suitcase landed on my left side, prompting me to turn in that direction. A staircase curved upwards, behind the row of shelves against the wall, almost hiding a darkened corridor.

"Our living quarters are through there," said Aunt Adelaide. "Private area, just for family."

"It mostly stays where it's supposed to," added Aunt Candace. "Also, only certain areas are open to the public, and if a door has an X on it, it's not to be opened without consulting one of us first."

My head spun like a merry-go-round. The place was beyond vast. I couldn't even see the ceiling above the endless stories of shelves. It was like being in a palace or castle—except filled with nothing but books. Their old-pages smell filled the air, and I inhaled deeply, swaying on the spot.

"Oh, is she going to faint again?" Aunt Candace said. "Aim for the floor, dear. The carpet's soft."

"I'm not going to faint," I said, my voice quiet in the open space. I'd spent most of my life around books, but this… this was something else entirely. The number of titles seemed as countless as the stars in the sky. Between the rows of shelves lay plush sofas, bean bags and chairs, more reading corners than I'd ever seen anywhere. It wasn't just vast, it was *alive,* filled with rustling sounds like the books were whispering to one another.

It put Abe's half-hearted decorating attempts to shame, that was for sure.

"I can give you a tour," said Estelle. "Only the ground floor. It's not fair to leave Cass on the front desk all day." She waved a hand in the direction of a gap between two of the towering stacks. I started, spotting other people sitting on the cushions, reading paperbacks, or climbing the ladders to reach the higher shelves. Nobody paid our group the slightest bit of attention. Apparently, a bunch of cloaked women appearing out of thin air was second nature in a place like this.

Between the shelves, old-fashioned lanterns floated unsupported, bathing the rich carpets in orange light. Ladders hovered off the ground, while books moved around unattended, flitting about like birds. Meanwhile, several pointy-eared people who came up to my waist were engaged in a whispered conversation, while a group of young women in bright pink cloaks occupied another corner, a book floating before them.

"We have strict rules on what spells can be used in the library," Estelle said in a low voice. "Academy students often come in here when it's too cold to practise outside."

I just nodded, utterly overwhelmed.

Estelle indicated the corridor behind the staircase. "As my mum said, this is our living quarters. We have our own rooms and an almost endless supply of guest rooms upstairs. The kitchen's downstairs, and the dining room. You'll stay in the room next to mine."

Estelle pulled out her wand and my suitcase rose into the air. I dragged my gaze away from the library and followed her up the narrow, winding staircase, which curved behind a bookcase. The staircase climbed to a long corridor painted in beige and carpeted in blue.

"This one," she said, pushing open the door on her left. The room was bare and sparsely furnished with oak wood furniture. An en-suite bathroom lay through a door on the right. My suitcase floated in and landed in the middle of the floor. I watched it, wondering once again what I'd got myself into. I was further out of my depth than I'd been when I'd waded into that river.

"Your other shelves will easily fit in here." Estelle put her wand back into one of the pockets of her long cloak. "And I'll help you liven the place up a bit later. Unless you want to unpack now?"

"Give her the tour," Aunt Candace called from downstairs. "I need to get back to my book."

"Of course you do." Estelle rolled her eyes. "Aunt Candace is an author. That's her real calling, as she tells us about seven times a day."

"Oh, that's awesome," I said, and meant it. "What sort of books does she write?"

"More like, what doesn't she write." Estelle grinned. "She has... five pen names now, isn't it? She won't always tell us what they are. We have to guess."

"Any reason for that?"

"She likes to experiment. Her fantasy capers are her best-known ones. Personally, I prefer the Adventures of Were-wolves in Cyberland, but she says it was a one-off."

"I prefer her romances," said Aunt Adelaide, walking onto the stairs to look up at us. "For someone who's as much of a romantic as a swamp goblin, she writes surprisingly sweet love stories."

"At least I don't date swamp goblins in real life," Aunt Candace said from behind her.

Aunt Adelaide turned pink. "He didn't specify in his profile beforehand."

Estelle said, "Don't you two start. Rory's freaked out enough as it is."

"I'm not," I lied. Hearing the group of them bicker like normal families was the closest to anything ordinary I'd seen since the shop door had opened and those vampires had come in. "So you all work full time here?"

"Yes, we do," said Estelle. "My mum runs the place, but the rest of us rotate jobs and do whatever needs doing. Speaking of, Cass isn't fond of dealing with people. I'll have to go and take over from her later, but there aren't too many people in here at the moment."

"Don't worry, we'll give you a little time to learn the basics before we put you to work," said Aunt Adelaide, with a smile. "We take it in turns and share all the tasks equally. It takes a joint effort to run the place."

"You said it was my grandmother's? The library?"

Aunt Adelaide's smile faded. "I'm sorry you never got to meet her, Rory. Your dad would have loved to bring her to see you as a baby, but she rarely left the library."

"She was a little eccentric," Estelle said. "Her husband—our grandfather—died before I was born. So now it's just us. Want to see it all?"

"I should take over from Cass," added Aunt Adelaide. "Before she and the goblin get into it again."

"Goblin?" I asked. There were goblins, too?

"Cass has a short fuse," said Estelle. "It's why we don't leave her to supervise the desk if we can help it. I'll show you around."

I left my rucksack beside my suitcase and followed Estelle back downstairs, weaving between the shelves to a spot with a clearer view of the towering stories. From here, the library's many floors resembled a layered cake or Christmas present, lit by floating lanterns.

"I love how it looks at night," Estelle said. "Grandma's the one who picked the lanterns. Aunt Candace wanted to replace them with electric lights, but I think it would wreck the atmosphere."

"So you do have electricity?" I asked. "I mean, in most of the fantasy books I've read, technology and magic are incompatible."

"Magic does have odd effects on some technology," she said. "But we have magical equivalents to almost everything. We've existed alongside normals for centuries, after all."

She resumed walking between the shelves. I tried to take in all the titles—*Divining Fates, Dining with the Dead, Conjuring for Beginners*—until I nearly walked headlong into a low-hanging hammock. A man wearing a lopsided green pointed hat lay sprawled on his back, snoring loudly. Estelle pressed a finger to her lips and sidestepped him, leading me around a spacious area between the shelves filled with bean bags, armchairs and cushions. A sign saying 'Reading Corner' floated between two lanterns.

The Reading Corner occupied the centre of the ground floor. Estelle led me around to the right-hand side and up a staircase to the first floor. Like the ground floor, a maze of shelves greeted us.

I stopped walking, overwhelmed. "Is there a map? Or signposts?"

"Ah, that's not really possible," she said. "That's why I wanted to give you this." She handed me a piece of paper with several words written on it. The first line said, *Exit.*

"If you get lost, hit that one," she said. "If you've been walking for more than an hour and haven't found any stairs, it'll take you back to the lobby."

"An *hour?*"

Her finger moved to the next word. *Help.* "That's the emergency alarm, but it's only meant to be used if your life is in danger. Again, it's best to call one of us by name if there's anything you need help with. Those words contain powerful magic. And if you want to find a particular section but can't find the way, you can ask one of us."

If your life is in danger? I'd ask what could possibly be dangerous about working in a library, but considering what I'd seen of the magical world so far... *I'll deal with that one later.*

I pocketed the paper, and a rustling noise behind me prompted me to turn around.

The staircase we'd come up was no longer there. Unfamiliar shelves stood on either side of us, forming a corridor with no way downstairs.

I turned to Estelle. "Did the shelves move?"

"The library does that," she said. "It's Grandma's fault. She's the one who created the place to be semi-sentient, after all."

"Wow, really?"

She nodded. "Her death was sudden and unexpected. Her will said that Aunt Candace and my mum were to inherit the library. What she *didn't* leave behind was a clear map or a set of directions as to everything she hid in here. Every few weeks, a visitor disappears in a hidden corridor or finds a room we've never found before. Keeps us on our toes, that's for sure. But it's home."

33

I realised my mouth was hanging open and closed it. "Wow. This is… a lot to take in."

"I bet it is," she said. "I'll take you back to your room and leave you in peace to unpack, okay? Ask me if you want to know anything more. I'll do my best to answer."

I had a list of questions as endless as the shelves, but I'd already overwhelmed myself enough times in one day.

Estelle led me on a different route back to my room. I tried to memorise the way, then told myself it was pointless if everything moved around. I'd just have to get used to being perpetually lost. Estelle kept glancing at me, perhaps wondering if I was going to faint again. I'd passed that point. I didn't even want to sleep. The smell of the books and the light of the lanterns would make me tired under normal circumstances, but my mind was awake and my eyes wide open. More so than I could remember in a long time.

Unpacking didn't take long. My aunts would fetch the rest of my possessions later, including the bookshelves, so I put away my clothes and unpacked the essentials.

Estelle was levitating paper birds down the corridor when I came out of my room.

"Ah, I was just practising," she said, snapping her fingers. The birds shot back into her hands, unfolding themselves into pieces of paper. "I'm doing a PhD in practical magic."

"Really?" I asked. Witches got PhDs? Whatever next?

She smiled. "Yes, I know it's not necessary when I have the library, but it's a fun project and it keeps me away from Cass's grumbling. It'll be nice to have a new witch around to brighten things up."

I didn't feel bright, even though I'd changed into jeans and T-shirt and hidden my former work clothes in the back of the wardrobe. The silver-lined black cloaks the others wore must be the library's uniform.

She caught me looking at her cloak and said, "Oh, that reminds me. I'll get you a cloak. Silver or blue lining?"

"Silver, please," I said. I wasn't keen on black, either, but they looked a thousand times more stylish than I had in my old work clothes. Not to mention the colour was appropriate to my new witchy existence. "No pointy hats?"

Estelle laughed. "No. Aunt Candace used to go through five hats a week. Things can go missing in here if you don't pay attention."

No kidding. Estelle bounded down the staircase—at least that one had stayed in the right place—into the corridor that led to the family's living quarters. Through one door was a kitchen, another led to a dining room, and a general living area lay beyond, complete with sofas and a TV. No wonder they'd been stunned at the size of my tiny one-room studio flat.

Estelle pulled a notebook and pen from her pocket—up close, both bore a similar silvery design—and wrote something in the book. There was a flash, and a cloak appeared draped over the sofa in front of us.

"I can get it adjusted to your size," she said. "Try it on."

I slid my arms into the sleeves. It was massive, but Estelle appraised me, wrote something in the book, and the cloak shrank, inch by inch, until it fitted me perfectly. It swept to ankle-length, far enough off the ground not to trip over the edge, and bore a silver crest symbol on the front.

"That's our family's coat of arms," she said, indicating the same symbol on her own cloak. The top of the coat of arms depicted two crossed wands—no, pens—and on the bottom, an owl sitting on top of an open book. "Grandma's design."

The same design was on her notebook and pen, too. I couldn't help thinking of the noticeable absence of family photos in my childhood home. I'd assumed it was because Mum had died when I was young and Dad had since removed all the pictures. Not that he was hiding an entire family. I imagined him sitting in the Reading Corner and swallowed a lump in my throat. He'd have been happy I'd found my way into this world. Right?

Estelle pocketed her pencil and notebook. "OkWant to see more of the library, or have a look at the town before it gets dark?"

"I'd like to see the town." Maybe I'd feel less disorientated if I knew what lay outside this giant maze of a library.

Estelle bounded out the door again. "Ivory Beach isn't at its best in winter. It's a coastal town, so we're not in tourist season at the moment, but lots of people come here just to see the library."

I followed her out of the family's living quarters and out into the library proper. We walked through the shelves, into the open area at the very front where Aunt Adelaide stood behind a large curved desk covered in stacks of books.

"Ah, good, Estelle set you up with your cloak," she said. "I was going to suggest you find something warm to wear if you're going outside."

"I'm just showing Rory the town square," Estelle said. "Cass didn't turn anyone into a frog while we were gone, did she?"

"Not this time," said Aunt Adelaide. "Come and help with the returns when you get back, okay?"

"Don't worry, we're not running off to the beach," said Estelle. "We won't be long."

She crossed to a set of oak wood doors and pushed them open. A sea breeze swept in, making me glad of the cloak, and the tinkling of a bell pursued us outside. The library sat on one side of a large town square, opposite a clock tower. Other, smaller shops filled the edges of the square.

"It looks a bit dull at this time of year," said Estelle. "Give it a week and there'll be Christmas trees everywhere."

"You celebrate Christmas in the magical world, then?"

"Oh, a lot of us follow the same traditions as normals, but embellished with a few of our own." She gestured to the row of shops on the left. "That's the bakery—I'll take you there tomorrow. Get you a late birthday cake if you want one."

I opened my mouth and closed it again, suddenly hit hard by how much had happened in a short space of time. Had I really turned twenty-five just yesterday?

Estelle was still talking, pointing out the various shops. "If you walk directly past the clock tower, you'll reach the sea. We have barbecues on the beach in summer if someone conjures up some nice weather. We have our own pier, too."

"You can magic up nice weather?" I gestured at the low-hanging grey clouds.

"Not permanently," she responded. "You might have trouble getting a tan, but my mum has a dozen spells for that."

"I spend all my time indoors," I said. "It's not a priority." I mean, I lived in England. I didn't exactly expect beach weather, even in the magical world. "Anyway, is everyone who lives here... paranormal?"

She nodded. "It's an isolated community. It's much easier that way. A lot of us experience side effects from being around humans too much, and in places like this, we can be ourselves."

I understood that. I imagined going back to tell Laney where I'd been for the last week without bringing up the impossibly magical library and drew a total blank.

"Side effects?" I asked. "I don't remember any. Unless the real reason we didn't get any customers is because I had a repelling spell on me."

"Nah, your dad will have used a spell that prevented any side effects," said Estelle. "He wanted you to have as normal a life as possible."

"Well, I guess I did, until today," I said. Normal? Absolutely. But there'd always been something missing, and now it rose within me—a wave of unexpected sadness. I'd had nobody after he died, and the others had all had each other.

"Are you okay?" Estelle asked.

"Oh, I'm fine," I lied, pushing the feeling aside. "Is the library where Dad grew up, then?"

"Yes, like the rest of us," she said. "Grandma more or less raised three kids single-handedly, since she lost her husband young. The library was her whole life."

I turned around to get a proper look at the place from the front. The library towered above the rest of the square, overlooking the town like a majestic monarch on a throne. Red bricks formed the exterior, set with stained-glass windows reflecting the setting sun. No wonder people came here just to see the library.

"Impressive," I said. "So I've met you all except Cass, right?"

"I'll introduce you," she said. "She tends to get a little... awkward around strangers."

"Oh, me too," I said. "As you might have gathered."

She smiled. "Actually, I think you're coping well, considering you've had your whole world upended. Don't expect to get the hang of everything right away."

"I'm a bit lost on how this biblio-witch thing works," I admitted. "I get that I can—write things and make them real. But how is that different to waving a wand?"

"All witches and wizards have one main talent," she said. "It's like a specialist area. Some can conjure up storms, others see into the future. Our family, though, we're special. We can all draw magic from words. Specialist talents tend to run in the family."

"And it's a rare thing?"

"We're the only family who can do it," she said. "That I know of, anyway."

"Oh, wow." That explained why they were so proud of their talents. And the library, too. "Is the library connected to our magic, then?"

"In a way," she said. "Grandma's magic created the place. That's what my mum said, anyway." She pulled out a small black book from her pocket. "This is the Biblio-Witch's Inventory. It contains all the spells we can do. Mum will set you up with one when you begin your training."

I glimpsed pages of handwritten words before she put it back into her pocket.

"As for wands," she went on, "you'll get one of those, too. Most people use wands to cast spells. We just have a second option. A better one, if I say so myself." She smiled. "There's no limit. With wands, you have to memorise movements and sometimes incantations. That's more complex. Biblio-Witchery is in your blood. You stopped a fire with a single word. You're a natural."

I hoped she was right. I scanned the town square, trying to commit it to memory. *My new home.* I hadn't had a fresh start in so long, but maybe it was for the best that I'd fallen headfirst into it. I tended to hover too long over making decisions and miss out. Not this time. Laney would be proud.

Speaking of... "Can I call my friends back home from here?"

"You might have trouble getting a signal, but once I get you hooked up to the paranormal network, you can call anyone outside the library," she said. "Same with the internet connection, but it works okay in our living quarters. The library's magic interferes everywhere else. To be honest, though, there's more than enough entertainment inside the library."

"The books, right?"

"Trust me, you're going to have the time of your life."

I hope you're right. Yet already, I felt more alive than I had in a long time. "Let's go back inside."

When we re-entered, it was to find a new face at the wide desk dominating the entrance. The young woman looked a little like Estelle but had longer hair and a willowy figure like Aunt Candace. The sleeves of her matching cloak were rolled up.

"Hey, Cass," said Estelle brightly.

Cass grunted. "Thanks for leaving me in charge. I had to chastise Samson over late fees *again,* and then a pixie got out of the Magical Creatures Division."

"Sorry, but it was an emergency," said Estelle. "Aurora— Rory—was being attacked by vampires."

Cass's gaze settled on me. "So you're Aurora."

"Yes." Her less-than-enthusiastic tone made me wary, but I pushed on. "It's great to meet you."

She shrugged. "Sure it is. Mum waltzed off and left me on the desk, but apparently her beauty routine is more important than the patrons staying in one piece."

"Cass!" Estelle said reproachfully. "Rory's had a tiring day and doesn't need to hear your complaining. She's new to the paranormal world."

"Really." Cass eyed me. "Fair warning, this place will sink its claws in you. Once you're here, you can never leave."

"We just did," I said. "Leave, I mean. Anyway, I hardly think being stuck here is a bad thing."

She gave a short laugh. "You'll see."

Well, then. I didn't need any of her negativity, so I walked past the desk, looking up at the stories of shelves. How could anyone live in a place like this and have a sour attitude like hers?

"Does she have a problem with me being here?" I asked Estelle, when we were out of earshot.

"It's not you specifically," said Estelle. "More like everyone. I'll ask her to behave herself at dinner. Meanwhile, I thought you might want to see some of the regulars."

She walked towards the Reading Corner we'd passed through before.

"That's Dominic." She pointed at an elegant-looking man standing on a ladder that looked far too tall to stand unsupported. At the sound of his name, he flashed us a smile, revealing pointed fangs.

My heart jumped. "He's a vampire?"

"Oh, he's harmless," she said.

Those pointed fangs didn't *look* harmless. I backed away from the ladder, wondering how in the world he expected to get down from such a high spot. Given how fast those vampires had moved, though, there was no doubt they had other tricks up their sleeves.

Estelle pointed to a younger man in the corner. He was maybe twenty or so with straw-like hair.

"That's Samson," she said in an undertone. "He comes here every day but never returns any of the books on time. It drives Cass out of her mind."

She moved on, pointing out each visitor, and I did my best to memorise all the names.

Finally, she reached a hammock at the back of the Reading Corner and said, "And that's Tad."

"And he's a wizard, right?" The man wore a bright green hat, which was positioned to cover his sleeping face.

She hesitated a moment. "Actually, as far as we know, he's not paranormal at all."

I glanced at the pointed hat. "But I thought the community was only for paranormals. No normals allowed."

The man woke with a start. "May the nefarious rites be fulfilled," he proclaimed.

"What does that mean?" I said blankly.

"He was put under a spell that addled his mind," she said in an undertone. "I don't know who did it, nobody does, but the town's best healers haven't been able to undo the damage. He'd be locked up in an asylum if he returned to the normal world, and it's not like he's in any fit state to give away our secrets."

Tad mumbled something intelligible and then fell asleep again. The paranormal world was far weirder than I'd initially thought—and that was saying a lot.

"Right," she said. "I have to take over from Cass, but we have an hour until dinner. Want to find something to read in the meantime? This is the fiction section."

I looked past the people at the surrounding bookcases. A thousand tomes gleamed on the shelves, as inviting as a feast. I grinned. "I reckon I can do that."

Cass might have been less than enthusiastic about my presence here, but I wasn't going anywhere. I'd had the most bizarre day of my life. The vampires had been terrifying, but meeting my family, seeing the library, the *magic?* I wouldn't have missed it for the world.

4

I woke early the following morning, after the best night's
sleep I'd had in what felt like years. Aunt Adelaide had
offered me a sleeping tonic at dinner and I'd accepted,
certain that my mind would start spinning in circles the
instant I lay down, reliving the rollercoaster of the day
before. Instead, I'd passed out for nine hours straight.

Dinner had been fairly quiet. Cass had spurned all my
attempts to make friendly conversation, so I'd settled for
talking to Aunt Adelaide and Estelle about my life with Dad
at the bookshop. It still hurt to imagine never seeing it again,
but I wouldn't end up on the streets. I had a job and a new
home, *and* a family. Not to mention access to more books
than I'd ever seen in my life. What more could I ask for?

Brightness shone through the blinds. They'd been closed
when I'd first come in and I hadn't got a good look outside,
but now I opened them, I could see past the clock tower to
the seafront. The tide was out, revealing a stony beach
running down to the sea. Sunlight streamed through the
clouds and glittered on the water.

Even if it'd been sunny every day, I'd have a hard time

tearing myself away from the library. I turned to my own bookshelves, which my aunts had transported here from home. My room looked bare compared to the rest of the place, but maybe I could decorate once I learned some magic.

I'd put Dad's journal on my bedside table, mostly to reassure myself it was still there. I'd yet to get any answers on why those vampires had been after it, but I'd been too preoccupied with the library to remember to ask Aunt Adelaide yesterday. She must know. It sounded like she'd been closer to Dad than Aunt Candace had.

I pulled a fresh outfit from my wardrobe to wear under my new cloak. Yesterday's clothes had already vanished from the bag marked 'laundry' overnight. Yet another perk of magic—no chores. Aunt Adelaide had reassured me I could live here rent-free, and I'd get a salary I could spend on anything I liked. It seemed too good to be true. Librarians didn't earn much in my experience, but this place was absurdly extravagant and my aunts had inherited it from Grandma. That suggested she'd had money, right? Another question for later. In the meantime, I dressed in a T-shirt and jeans—no more bookshop uniform for me—and put on my cloak before opening the door.

I'd thought Estelle's room was next to mine, but there weren't any other doors at all. Just blank walls. Odd. Closing the door behind me, I walked slowly down the corridor. My room had only one exit, so I must be in the right place. I turned the corner. Still no doors, and no stairs leading down into the family's living quarters, either. Instead, an unfamiliar staircase spiralled upwards. That hadn't been there yesterday. I'd have knocked on Estelle's door to ask her, but it wasn't there.

The staircase stopped after one spiral and had no door at the top, only a blank wall. *Huh?*

A rustling noise came from above my head, and a large

bird flew down, feathers tickling my face. I stumbled back, stifling a yelp of surprise. A large tawny owl hovered in front of me, its head rotating so it was looking at me backwards.

"Hello," said the owl, in a loud, male voice.

My heart jumped in my chest. "You can talk!"

"Wow, you're not a very bright one, are you?" His eyes scanned me, then his head rotated the right way around and he looked me up and down again. "Definitely a biblio-witch, though. That makes you the lost cousin Aurora, correct?"

"Well, I *am* lost at the moment," I admitted. "Do you have a name?"

"Sylvester," he said. "And you're Aurora."

"I go by Rory," I said. "Most of the time. Is the library rearranging things again? This staircase wasn't here before."

"It certainly was the last time *I* checked," said the owl. "If the staircase isn't here, then neither am I. Maybe none of us are here."

I tried to think that one through and gave up before it gave me a headache. I'd rather not have a philosophical debate with an owl when I hadn't even had coffee yet. "Where's the way downstairs?"

"Someone's got a sharp tongue," he observed, clucking his beak at the emblem on my new cloak. "That same someone is dressed in our uniform. That makes you a biblio-witch, which makes you an expert on the library. It looks like our standards are slipping."

"That's not a nice thing to say. I am new here. Who even are you, anyway?"

"I'm your family's familiar, of course," he said self-importantly. "I help run the place. Meaning Adelaide and I run the place, because Candace is about as much help as a used teabag."

"That's not a nice thing to say, either," I said.

"Did I ever claim to be nice, Aurora?" He spread his wings

45

wider, and I backed up a few steps. I'd never been a huge fan of birds, not since a swan had nearly bitten off my finger when I was a kid.

"Nope," I said. "We've clarified that you're not nice and I'm lost. What do you do, chase the guests?"

He clucked his beak. "I work for the library. That means I'm in charge of late fees."

"But of course. Can you please point me in the direction of the stairs down to the kitchen?"

"Wouldn't that spoil the fun?" He took flight up the staircase, disappearing in a rustle of wings.

Great. The staircase appeared to be the only way out, but it ended in a blank wall, which the owl had apparently flown through.

I *really* needed coffee. I turned the corner and walked back to my room. Past the door, the corridor didn't finish at a dead end as I first thought. Instead, there was no wall, just... nothing. I peered over the carpeted floor at the sheer drop. Was there anywhere to land?

"I wouldn't advise it."

I jumped, almost tripping over the carpet's edge.

"Clumsy *and* slow." Sylvester fluttered down to my side.

"How did you get back in?" I asked. "You flew... through a wall. Which is also impossible, I might add."

"Not only are you slow, you have no imagination whatsoever."

"There's nothing wrong with my imagination," I protested. "Just where I come from, the world obeys basic rules."

"Oh, *does* it?" He clucked his beak. "How dull. I do hope you get what you came here for."

He took flight in a flutter of wings. Shaking my head, I peered over the edge. There must be a way down. When I leaned right over, I saw the corridor which led to the family's living quarters below, as though someone had removed the stairs.

"Rory?" Estelle's voice drifted from downstairs. "Where are you?"

"On a ledge," I called.

She came out of one of the doors below and looked up at me. "Oh, did the library move the stairs again? It's usually better with strangers, but I probably should have warned it that someone new was staying overnight."

"No worries," I said, as though I dealt with semi-sentient libraries every day. "I also met Sylvester, but he wasn't much help at getting me un-lost."

"Oh, him," she said. "Sorry, he makes Cass look positively welcoming."

"That's one way of putting it. He said he was the family's familiar?"

"He is," she said. "I was on my way to grab breakfast—I slept in a bit late, so we'll be opening soon. Want anything?"

"Er, a way down?" I said. "Sorry, I haven't had any coffee yet."

Estelle pulled out her pen and notebook. "Oh, are you like Aunt Candace? She can't function on less than a pot of coffee —there."

The ledge flickered and became a staircase leading down into the corridor. I stepped onto it warily, but it felt solid enough. Still, I climbed down as fast as I could in case it decided to vanish again.

In the main part of the library, the lanterns weren't lit yet, but the sun through the stained-glass windows bathed the carpet in bright colours.

"Wow," I said. "This place is atmospheric."

"Isn't it?" She beamed. "That's why it's the most popular venue for hire. It adapts to every occasion. We've even had wedding receptions here."

"Seriously?" I asked.

She nodded. "My official title is head of hospitality when I'm not handling the day-to-day running of the library. Of course, my mum's meant to be in charge of that, but sometimes things get away from her."

"Like the stairs?"

Estelle grinned. "Yes, like the stairs. And the floors sometimes, too."

I peered after her into the kitchen. Unlike the rest of the library, it wasn't filled with books, but the appliances looked modern. "What's on the menu for breakfast?"

"Whatever you like, within reason," she said, opening cupboards. "How about one of these? Breakfast bars with an energy boost. I think you might need it today."

"Sounds good."

She pulled out two bars and passed one to me as we walked through into the main living area, where someone had left three steaming mugs out on the coffee table. Estelle picked up one and sniffed it.

"Mood-boosting coffee," she said. "I'd guess the third one's for Cass."

She took a seat on the sofa, which looked identical to the one my aunts had transported over to my flat yesterday.

"Does your mum think I need my mood boosting?" I picked up the nearest mug and took a sip. Tasted like normal coffee to me.

"Nah, but Cass does," Estelle said.

"Do I have to pay for any of this?" I asked, taking a bite from the bar. The taste of apple and cinnamon filled my mouth.

"Oh, no, everything in the kitchen is for whoever gets there first," she explained. "If you want to buy food from outside the library, you can use your earnings—my mum's sorting that out for you."

When I'd finished my breakfast, I said, "I need to make a phone call."

"Ah, use our phone," Estelle said. "We'll add your phone to the paranormal network so you can make calls and access the internet. I'll do that when I have a free moment."

"Right, you said sometimes magic can interfere with technology."

"More like the library," she said. "Some technology used by normals often breaks or malfunctions, which is why you won't see many cars here. The town's small enough to get around on foot, so it's not a huge issue. And we have transportation spells."

Then I wouldn't be visiting home for a while. Calling Laney would bring back all my bad feelings about being fired, but it wasn't fair to ditch her, so I drew on all the fortitude from the mood-boosting coffee and went over to the phone on the sideboard.

I dialled Laney's number, cobbling together my story.

"Hello?" she said. "Who is this?"

Right—she wouldn't know the number I was calling from.

"It's me, Rory," I said.

"Rory!" she shrieked. "Thank god, I thought you were in trouble. Alice said she saw some strange men outside your flat."

"Oh. Yeah." *They'd better leave my friends alone.* "Long story short, I got fired. Abe kicked me out."

Her breath caught. "Oh, I'm so sorry, Rory. What will you do?"

"I'm okay," I said. "I... this is going to sound crazy, but it turns out my dad had two sisters who I never met. They've been out of contact with the family. But they found me, and well, offered me a chance to live with them."

"Really?"

49

"Yeah, they have their own family business and I can work there while I get back on my feet. They own a library, can you believe it?"

She positively squealed. "I'll have to come and visit."

Oh, no. The non-paranormal rules...

"This is all new to me," I said quickly. "I'm just getting to know my new family. But I'll ask my aunts."

"Oh, of course, you only moved this week," she said. "But it sounds perfect for you. Call me soon and let me know how it goes."

"I will," I said. "I'll talk to you soon."

"Absolutely." She hung up, leaving me feeling like the worst best friend in the world. But I didn't even know how far from home I'd travelled. At least an hour, since Ivory Beach lay on the coast.

Estelle gave me a questioning look. "Are you okay?"

"Laney is... she's my best friend. We haven't seen a lot of each other in the last few years, but she'll be upset if I disappear without ever contacting her again."

Estelle pursed her lips. "Ask my mum. She can manufacture a cover story or even arrange for you to meet her somewhere else. There's no limit when it comes to magic."

I turned those words over in my head. All my life, I'd run into limits. Dad hadn't been rich, and I'd had to spend my inheritance on the deposit for my flat. Then for the last three years, all I'd done was scrape by. I'd worked all the time. My social life had been mediocre. Now I had a new job I could learn to love, and no more Abe underpaying and belittling me.

Propelled by the mood-boosting coffee, I walked with Estelle into the main area of the library. Without the lights, it seemed to contain twice as many shadowy corners than before, but it didn't look unwelcoming or scary.

Sylvester swooped overhead, landing on a nearby shelf. "Found your way off the stairs, did you?"

"Sylvester!" said Estelle. "Don't wind up Rory. Be nice."

I turned away from the owl. "Will I get my own familiar?"

"Oh, you might," she said. "All four of us share Sylvester, but it's not typical. The library isn't animal friendly and even magical animals get spooked easily."

"Because they lack imagination." Sylvester took flight in a flutter of wings.

"Is that his go-to insult?" I asked.

"One of them," she said. "Okay, we'll do the returns. I think Cass left some from yesterday."

I walked after Estelle with a new spring in my step, eager to see more of the library. "Where do I begin?"

"Here." She stopped beside a floating box near the front. "Returns go in here. There's a dozen magical ways to return them to their proper places, but some require special handling. This'll give you the chance to get to know the library, besides."

"Works for me." I smiled.

Estelle handed me a long roll of paper. "This tells you the codes we use and the sections they correspond to. I won't pretend it's straightforward, but sorting the books into the right piles is a good starting point." She pointed at the floating box, which levitated itself over to the wide desk at the front and tipped upside-down. A handful of books fell out, and Estelle picked one up. She showed me the spine, which was marked with a sticker telling me it belonged in Section D12. I checked it against the list and found it was the 'Potions and Poisons' section.

Aunt Adelaide called Estelle's name, and she turned around. "I bet she wants me to fetch Cass. If you need help reaching the higher shelves, call Sylvester. He might complain a lot, but he takes his job seriously and he always comes when you call his name."

"Okay, sure." I was less than enthused at the idea of working with the owl, but if we were going to be living in the same library, I might as well try to reason with him. I hadn't seen Cass yet either. After her attitude yesterday, I couldn't say I was disappointed. Dealing with Sylvester would be enough on its own. "Where's the Potions and Poisons section?"

"Third floor," said a self-important voice, and Sylvester fluttered down to land on the book pile. "Watch the books. Some of them bite."

"Ha ha." I resisted the impulse to check the book I was holding for sharp teeth. Estelle would have mentioned if I was in danger of losing a finger to a paperback. "I take it the sections generally stay in the right place? It'll stay on the third floor?"

Sylvester clucked his beak and didn't answer. Figuring I'd work it out as I went along, I headed for the staircase on the right, which curved above the entryway with an exit on each floor.

I reached the third floor without anything weird happening and stopped to admire the view of the sprawling ground floor from three stories up.

"Are you going to return the book or stand there gawking at the view?" Sylvester enquired.

I gave him a scowl. "Both. Not all of us have wings."

I made my way through to the second corridor. The Potions and Poisons section was full of ominous stains and odd smells, but I managed to locate the right spot without needing to call Sylvester back in. One of the books hissed at me on the way out, but I ignored it. Hissing was fairly harmless, all things considered.

The next one was trickier. I had a single book to return

to the Dimensional Study section, which seemed to rest somewhere between the second and third floors. I walked up and down different staircases for ten minutes before I found one that stopped off at the right section. The instant my foot hit the ground, the shelves moved to the left. I stepped down on my right foot, and the shelves moved again.

Okay...

I checked the number on the spine, turned to the right, and the shelves shifted to the side as though they were on an invisible conveyer belt. Every time I tried to read the number on the side, the shelves did another shuffle.

"Stop!" I commanded.

To my surprise, the shelves rolled to a halt. I ran three rows down to the right section, reaching to slide the book into place. To my annoyance, the shelves shifted upwards, out of reach.

"Oh, come on."

I stood on tip-toe and the shelves shifted yet again. When I grabbed the ladder, the shelves climbed higher. A rustling sounded from the pages. If I didn't know better, the books were laughing at me.

I fixed on a glare. "Stop it. I might be new, but I live here now. Let me put the book back."

To my surprise, the shelf dropped a couple of levels, so I put the book onto the shelf. Immediately, the shelves lurched to the right and started their conveyer belt act again. I turned my back and walked to the stairs.

Problem: the stairs were gone. Oh, no. They must have moved along with the shelves.

I turned to the side. The shelves kept moving—not just up and down and left to right, but in an oddly rippling manner that made my eyes glaze over and completely blocked any possible paths between the shelves. I looked down at the floor, then wished I hadn't. The blue spirals on the carpet were moving, too.

I have to get out. With no staircase, the only way to go was forwards until the library took pity on me and let me out.

My head spun with vertigo, so I closed my eyes and flat-out sprinted. Rustling and clicking pursued me. I opened my eyes—too late. Both my feet went *through* the top step of the staircase.

"Ah!"

My hand snagged on the edge of the second stair. Only the first one had vanished, but both my legs had disappeared through the gap and I couldn't see how deep the drop was.

Sylvester fluttered down to land on the bannister. "You could have asked for my help."

"I didn't know if you'd come into that section." I gripped the stairs with both hands, my heart thumping.

"Are you joking?" He gave a hoarse laugh. "As if I'd miss the chance to see your first encounter with the Dimensional Study Section."

I sucked in a breath. "Can you help me out of here?"

"No," he said. "You're too heavy for me to lift."

I pulled myself up, wincing when my knee got stuck halfway out of the stairs.

Sylvester laughed, his wings fluttering as he collapsed into hysterics in mid-air. I made a rude gesture at him, saying farewell to all attempts at being civil. "I'm glad you get so much entertainment out of my misfortune."

He stopped cackling and said, "Well, *now* I won't help you."

Did this count as an emergency? I'd grab the paper Estelle had given me with the emergency words, but I couldn't reach my pocket from this angle. I lowered my leg so my knee was no longer jammed and pulled myself out onto the second stair. Gripping the bannister with shaking hands, I practically flew down the remaining stairs and found Estelle near the table where I'd left the other books.

"Rory, you look frazzled. What happened?"

"The Dimensional Study Section happened."

She winced. "Oh, no. Sorry, I should have taken that one."

"No worries," I said. "It's kind of my own fault. I tried to run through with my eyes closed and accidentally fell through the stairs. Sylvester found it hilarious."

"I'll have a word with him," she said. "He might be a bit caustic, but I reckon he's channelling Cass."

"He's still nicer than my old boss," I said. 'By a fraction, anyway."

"Still," she said. "Tell you what—want to help me tidy the Reading Corner before it gets busy? This is the family friendly area. No hidden surprises."

"Sure," I said. Though I had an inkling the magical world's definition of 'family friendly' might differ from mine. The Reading Corner was deserted aside from Tad, who lay in his usual hammock wearing the same green pointed hat as yesterday.

"We're not that busy yet, but things pick up around lunchtime," she said. "We have a free snack bar. Helps keep the shifters happy. Ah, speaking of…"

Someone had entered through the front door, which made a tinkling noise. Estelle turned in that direction. "People are always arriving early," she said in an undertone. "Cass isn't around yet. Hey, Lucy," she said.

"Hey," said the young woman who'd just come in. "Have you got anything on Paranormal Laws? I'm late with an assignment again."

"Ah, that'll be in the reference section here on the ground floor," she said. "It's by the Reading Corner. Tell you what, you go and find it, Rory. It's Section A14."

"Okay." I might have had a less than stellar introduction

to the upper floors, but I liked the Reading Corner, with its soft lanterns and comfy seats.

I walked through to the Reading Corner and checked the shelf numbers. A14 was to the left, so I went that way. The shelves stayed where they were, and there was a single copy of the book I needed. I reached and pulled it off the shelf, tucked it under my arm, and something caught my eye. On my right, a foot poked from between the shelves. A human foot.

I trod closer. A man lay between the shelf and its neighbour, on his side, a book clasped in his hands.

"Er… excuse me?"

No response came. My heart kick-started, and I whirled to face the Reading Corner. "Hey! Can someone get over here?"

A goblin looked up at me and hurried over. "Is that Duncan?"

The man didn't move or answer. The goblin moved to his side, then recoiled.

"He's dead," he said.

5

E stelle was at my side in an instant, her hand clasped to her mouth. "Oh, no."

The library might have no end of surprises, but a dead body was evidently *not* a normal occurrence.

"Someone call Aunt Adelaide." She crouched down over his body, pulling out a thick, padded book with a dark plain cover. Opening the book, she tapped the page, muttering under her breath. "I think he was cursed. It's not coming up with a natural cause of death."

"When did he die?" I asked. "He was hidden back here, between those two shelves."

"It must have been today," said Estelle. "An hour ago at most. Someone would have seen otherwise. I wouldn't think he stayed overnight. Has anyone left in the last hour?"

"No," Sylvester said, perching on the shelf. For once, his smug expression was absent. "Nobody has. That means the murderer is in the library right now, in all likelihood."

I stared at the man's body, my heart hammering. He was about my age, maybe a bit younger, with thick dark hair and eyebrows and pale skin. His eyes were open, his hands still clasping the heavy-looking book to his chest. I knelt to look at it. "What's that book he's holding?"

"Don't touch it!" Estelle said. "It's a magical item. I'm almost certain it caused his death."

"But—that's one of our books," I said. "Look at the spine." It bore the same labelling system as the other books, along with our family's coat of arms.

"Make room," said Aunt Adelaide, sailing through the gathering crowd towards us. "What happened? Did anyone see?"

A few murmurs followed. Nobody had seen. The few patrons present—aside from Tad, who'd slept through the whole thing—all gathered around my aunt, muttering anxiously.

"It looks like a magical cause of death, since there isn't a mark on him," Estelle said. "We should call the police, but it's definitely a witch or wizard's work."

Who'd pick a library as the place to commit murder? Admittedly, the labyrinthine shelves offered endless places to hide a body, but the killer had chosen a spot right next to the Reading Corner. As opposed to, say, the Dimensional Studies Section. Not the act of someone who wanted to hide their crime.

I scanned the patrons. One, I recognised from yesterday, the vampire called Dominic. The memory of those creepy vampires was fresh in my mind, but Estelle had said it was a witch or wizard who'd committed the murder and I trusted her judgement more than mine.

The doorbell rang, making me jump. Were the police here already? I headed that way to see, and a man strode in through the doors. He had startling white-blond hair, and he held a long, curved weapon over his shoulder.

Nobody moved to stop him. The breath froze in my

lungs. *Are they seriously going to let him walk in here carrying that... weapon?*

Worse, his eyes were fixed on me. I should move, but my legs had turned to lead weights. The man kept walking until we stood face to face. His eyes were a clear shade of blue-green, striking against his dark clothes.

"Can I help you?" I asked.

"I am the Reaper," he said. "And I'm here to collect."

My heart missed a beat. "The Reaper... as in the Grim Reaper?"

"Yes," he said. "You're new here, right?"

He moved the sword—no, *scythe*—off his shoulder and gripped it in both hands.

"Don't take my soul!" I squeaked.

"Oh, you're not the one I'm here for," he said. "There's a body in here, isn't there? I sensed it."

Because that wasn't creepy at all. Still, at least it wasn't my soul he was after. "This way," I said, beckoning him towards the Reading Corner. I wished he'd lower that weapon of his. What in the world was he planning to do with it?

Despite his ominous presence, nobody seemed surprised to see him, and the crowd parted to let the Reaper through.

"Oh, Xavier, you're here," said Aunt Adelaide. "Good. We're having trouble identifying the cause of death. It's certainly magical, but..."

The Reaper—Xavier—stood for a moment, holding the scythe over the man's body. His brow furrowed. "His soul is gone."

A shocked hush fell over the patrons. Even Aunt Adelaide paled.

"What does that mean?" I whispered to Estelle.

"It means he was killed by a curse," said Aunt Candace, striding into view. "A dark curse."

Everyone watched as Aunt Candace approached, her wild

hair standing on end and an almost excited bounce to her steps.

"But—" Estelle stopped. "If a wand killed him, someone would have seen or heard. His body's right next to the Reading Corner."

"Precisely," said Aunt Candace. "Unless, of course, the curse was cast on an object." Her gaze went to the book.

"She's right," Aunt Adelaide said. "It needs to be quarantined immediately."

"There's one small problem," said the Reaper. "I was sent here to collect a soul. I can't leave without it. It's the rules."

Oh, no. Did that mean he'd have to take someone else in exchange? I looked away from his gaze. Surrendering my soul to the Reaper had *not* been on my to-do list for my first day here.

Seeing me staring, Estelle moved closer. "That means he has to stay until we find out where Duncan's soul went. It's not possible for it to just *disappear.*"

"I'll take your word for it," I whispered. "I've never even seen a dead body before."

The Reaper was still watching me, his head tilted. I wished he'd put the scythe away if he wasn't going to use it.

The doorbell rang again, and this time, a small man with pointed ears walked over to the Reading Corner. He wore a blue uniform with a silver badge.

"That's Edwin," said Estelle. "He leads the local law enforcement."

Edwin approached Estelle, giving me an appraising look. "You're unfamiliar. New in town?"

"I'm Aurora," I said. "I'm the new assistant here— Estelle's my cousin and Adelaide is my aunt. So is Candace."

Cass was still noticeably absent. Sylvester refrained from making a comment on my discovery of Duncan's murder, to my relief. I'd already found a dead body—I didn't need to be accused of putting it there.

Edwin looked around. "Tell me what happened here."

"We found Duncan's body in there, between the shelves," said Estelle, pointing. "Xavier just told us he's unable to collect his soul, since it's gone. That suggests a powerful curse caused his death."

"Yes, it does," said Aunt Adelaide. "However, it wasn't done with a wand."

"We think it's in the book he's holding," added Estelle. "There's a strong possibility it might not be safe to touch."

"No, well, that's your area of expertise," said the elf, stopping at a suitable distance from the man's corpse. "Take care of the book and I'll have my people remove the body. Who found him?"

All eyes turned to me. My mouth went dry. "I did," I said. "Someone hid his body between those two shelves, like Estelle said."

"You found him," he said. "The newcomer."

"She can't use much magic yet," Estelle said quickly. "She's new in town. Just found out she was paranormal yesterday."

More murmurs broke out. I spoke over them. "It's true. I was on my way to find a book and found him lying there. Whoever put him here must have hoped nobody would find him until after they left."

"Unluckily for them," said Aunt Candace, "Sylvester has been watching the door all morning. All the possible culprits are here in this room."

"Exactly," said the owl, fluttering his wings and drawing everyone's attention. "Nobody left."

"Oh, Cass must be somewhere upstairs," added Aunt Candace. "Someone can fetch her, and I'll remove that book."

"That book is police property," said Edwin.

"Do you want to be cursed?" Aunt Candace enquired.

Aunt Adelaide shot her a warning look. "What my sister means to say is that the book is likely still afflicted with the curse that killed Duncan. In the interests of safety, it should remain here. Books are our area of expertise, after all. It wouldn't be the first cursed book we've held at our establishment."

"Evidently," the elf said, with another glance at me. "Would any of you have reason to murder that man? You knew him? Regular visitor, was he?"

"He was," said Aunt Adelaide. "I'll talk to you—Candace, please put the book in quarantine. The quicker we figure out the curse, the easier it will be to trace the caster."

She steered Edwin to the side to speak to him, and to my surprise, he went along without a fuss. My family must know the police well. Then again, the library was at the town's centre, Estelle had said.

"None of you move," Aunt Candace snapped at the others. "Sylvester, see to it that nobody wanders off. Now, let me work my magic."

She pulled out a plain black book like the one Estelle had used and tapped a page with her fingertip. The dead man's hands moved, releasing the book he held, which levitated into the air. Chains appeared and wrapped around the book, sealing it closed.

"What *is* that?" I asked.

"Protection. Just in case." Aunt Candace waved a hand, and the book floated through the middle of the crowd. Everyone ducked out of the way. "I'll put it in one of the classrooms. I don't know what'll happen when I try to crack it open, but I'd advise you to avoid the general area for a bit."

"But who's the man who died?" I asked. His arms had collapsed to his sides after he'd let the book go, but there still wasn't a mark on him. His eyes were wide open, his jaw slack. *His soul is gone,* Xavier had said.

"Duncan," Estelle said. "He was a student at the town's University of Spellcraft. Pretty harmless. I can't think why anyone would try to kill him."

"Some of us wanted to at his poetry readings," said Cass, appearing behind her.

"Cass!" said Estelle.

"Poetry readings?" I asked.

"They're a weekly feature here at the library, every Monday evening," Estelle explained. "Very popular. And yes, Duncan showed up every week with a new poem. Bad poetry is not an excuse to curse someone, though."

Cass snorted. "Depends if you came to the last one or not. 'Ode to the Decapitated Rat My Cat Brought In' made me want to write my own obituary."

Someone was displaying an alarming lack of sympathy for the dead.

The sleeping man in the hammock woke with a start. "Let the nefarious rites begin," he proclaimed, startling everyone in the vicinity. Like me, they'd forgotten he was there.

"What does that mean?" I asked.

"In time you'll learn not to ask that question," said Cass. "Assuming you stick around. Personally, I wouldn't if I were in your position, even without the dead body."

"Cass," Estelle said warningly. "Well, it's safe to say Tad didn't do it, he doesn't even know his own name. The police will want to question the others…"

"Yes, we would," Edwin said. "Starting with the person who discovered the body."

I swallowed. Maybe it wasn't the Reaper I should have been worried about after all.

Aunt Adelaide gave me an encouraging nod as I followed the elf policeman through one of the many open doors to the left of the Reading Corner and into what appeared to be a classroom. He took a seat. So did I.

"So, you're new here," Edwin said. "Know anything about curses?"

I shook my head. "No. I know that there are different types of magic and I'm a biblio-witch. That's it."

"Like your family," he said. "Luckily for you, your family's library is the centre of the town. They're very well respected, and they often help us handle crimes involving little-known magic. This one will be no different. It's a shame that the murder took place here, however, especially with a newcomer in town."

"I didn't know the man who died," I said. "And I wouldn't know how to go about cursing a book even if I wanted to. Is the Reaper going to stay here until Aunt Candace finds his soul?"

He tapped his fingertips on the desk. "The Reaper? Considering the nature of the curse, I've no doubt he'll help you get to the bottom of it."

I wasn't sure how I was supposed to react. Most people didn't want to spend a lot of time with the Grim Reaper, right?

"You found the body between the shelves, correct?" he went on. "Was Duncan holding the book?"

"He was," I said. "Until my aunt removed it, anyway. I didn't touch him."

"Good," he said. "Since you're new, you won't know the signs of magical contamination. Your aunt will handle the book. You can leave, Aurora. And welcome to Ivory Beach."

I let the room, relieved that Edwin hadn't seemed to think I was guilty. Then again, as Sylvester had implied, I had 'newbie' written all over me.

While Edwin called Estelle over for questioning, I joined Aunt Adelaide in the Reading Corner. The other patrons sat in the various armchairs and perched on bean bags and in hammocks. There were three goblins, two elves and a vampire. The rest looked human, so they must be witches and wizards—with the exception of Tad, who appeared to have fallen asleep again.

"I'm sorry, Rory," Aunt Adelaide said as I took a seat on the bean bag beside her. "I didn't know he'd question you first."

"Don't worry about it," I said. "I might have found the body, but I wouldn't know a curse if it hit me. Let alone how to steal someone's soul. I didn't even know souls existed, to tell you the truth."

"That's my area," said Xavier, from behind my seat, startling me. I hadn't even seen him move. "Normally my job is straightforward. Even most murders end with the soul where it's supposed to be."

"Uh… is murder really that common here?" I asked.

"No," said Aunt Adelaide. "Accidents are, though."

"Especially in the library," Cass put in. She sat on a bean bag with a book open in her lap. "This place is dangerous for the unprepared. Curses are in every other room. I doubt they'll find who did it."

"Ignore her," Estelle said, taking a seat on my right. Dropping her voice, she added, "She's in a foul mood because she split up with her boyfriend over the weekend. He left town, so the rest of us are getting the brunt of her annoyance instead."

"Fun." I looked up at the sound of rustling. Sylvester perched on the top of the shelf behind Cass, watching everyone with his large owl-eyes.

"Edwin is a decent police chief," said Aunt Adelaide. "Lucky he is, and very lucky he works so closely with the library. This could have gone very badly if it were otherwise."

"Yeah, he said you sometimes help the police out," I said.

"We're a close community in Ivory Beach," she said. "With

all the knowledge we have in here, we often find ourselves able to help where others fail."

"So... only a witch or wizard could have cursed the book?" I asked.

"Yes," Aunt Adelaide confirmed. "However, a non-witch or wizard might have hired or asked someone else to do it. That's why the police want to question us individually. It's likely someone who knew Duncan personally was responsible."

Cass snorted. "Well, half the town had to suffer through the last poetry night."

"Cass! Estelle!" Aunt Candace's voice drifted from between the bookshelves. "I need your help in here."

Cass shrugged and jumped off the bean bag while Estelle got to her feet. I followed them to another open classroom door. The room was free of furniture and Aunt Candace stood in the centre, her pen and notebook in her hands. The book Duncan had been holding floated in the middle of a glowing circle on the room's floor.

"That's a protective ward," said Estelle. "It'll stop the book from harming us if it turns out the curse is on the book."

"But—hang on," I said. "If the book's cursed, how did it end up in Duncan's hands? If it kills everyone it touches, the murderer couldn't have handled it, right?"

Cass made a disparaging noise, but Aunt Candace gave an approving nod. "She's right. That means he might not have been the intended target. If I was going to murder someone, I'd have put the curse on one of their personal possessions, not a book that belonged to a public library."

"Please don't say that in front of the police," said Aunt Adelaide. "However—yes, Duncan might not have been the intended target."

"Any of us might have been the target," said Cass, with a not-so-subtle glance at me. "Still sure you want to live here?"

"Cass!" said Aunt Adelaide. "That's no way to speak to your cousin."

"It's best she learns that lesson early," Cass said. "Rather than having a nasty surprise later down the line."

"If you don't want to work here, why not leave?" I asked her.

"I never said *I* didn't want to work here."

Aunt Candace scribbled in her notebook, then she got out the black-covered book she'd used beforehand. To my surprise, Cass reached into her pocket and pulled out an identical book, albeit one that looked smaller. The two of them opened their books and spoke the same word at once: *Reveal.*

The word reverberated through my body, along with a rush of wild energy. The book floating in the middle of the circle glowed around the edges but didn't move.

"Excuse me?" Edwin said from behind us.

"What?" snapped Aunt Candace.

"I need to question you," said the chief of police.

"Can't you see we're busy?" she said.

"My sister means that she's on the verge of undoing that curse," added Aunt Adelaide.

"It might take a while." Aunt Candace pocketed the book again. "Fine, do the questioning here."

Edwin looked somewhat put out. "Do you have an alibi for where you were when Duncan died?"

"I was on the second floor," said Aunt Candace.

"Can anyone confirm that?"

"Let me think... no."

Aunt Adelaide groaned. "Sorry, she's a little absent-minded when she's highly focused on a task."

"We all know who did it, anyway," Cass said.

"Would you mind enlightening me?" the elf asked haughtily. It seemed he didn't care much for Cass either.

"Isn't it obvious?" Cass said. "Dominic made no secret of the fact that he despised Duncan's poetry. He brought a whole group of vampires to the last poetry night to make fun."

A whole group of vampires? I shivered at the thought.

"Oh, he's harmless." Aunt Candace gave Cass a disgruntled look. "He's never bitten anyone on our property without permission."

Estelle caught my arm and whispered, "Let's get out of here."

We left the crowded room and returned to the Reading Corner. My gaze went to Dominic immediately, taking him in for the first time. He sat back in one of the armchairs, reading a newspaper. Like the other vampires I'd encountered, his features were eerily handsome, yet sort of... frozen. His face was expressionless, and he sat still, not a muscle twitching. Cass thought he'd killed Duncan? He sure *looked* creepy, and after my narrow escape yesterday, it was hard to look at him and not remember the terror of being cornered. But I had no business judging total strangers.

"Don't worry," Estelle said quietly. "Cass is just being... Cass. Personally, I don't think anyone in this room is likely to have killed him. Vampires can't use magic."

"But they can bite people."

Dominic glanced up from his newspaper and I tensed. I was too far for him to hear me, right?

"Not legal," she muttered. "Also, they have enhanced senses and can read minds, so er, you might want to bring it up when he's not so close."

"Oh." That's why he was looking at me. I averted my gaze, flushing. "Mind-reading?"

"Yes, most vampires can do it," she said. "It's a bit unnerving, but we're used to it. Their powers are restricted to anyone in the same room as them. I think it might be linked to eye contact, too, but they're pretty tight-lipped on the subject."

That must be how those strangers had known my name. Before they'd arrived at the shop, they'd expected my dad, not me. Until they'd seen me and read the truth straight from my mind.

I shoved the memory aside, with difficulty. We had more pressing matters to concern ourselves with. Like the murder. Not everyone had alibis. Cass and Aunt Candace hadn't been around, for one. I hoped they wouldn't say anything unfortunate during the questioning. Part of me couldn't help wondering if the killer had wanted one of the library's owners to take the blame.

"What's the book that killed him, do you know?" I asked Estelle. "I didn't get a good look at the cover."

"That's the weird part," she said. "It's a book of curses."

6

T he book of curses remained shut despite Aunt Candace's best efforts. While the chief of police called each of the other people in the Reading Corner in for questioning, Estelle and I went to see how our aunt was getting along.

Aunt Candace faced the floating book with a scowl on her face. She didn't appear to have made any progress. The book itself was unremarkable, bound in leather with yellowed pages.

"How can someone put a curse on a book of curses?" I asked. "Wouldn't they need to *read* the book to use the curse?"

"I assume they got what they needed then sealed the damned thing shut," said Aunt Candace. "Unfortunately for all of us, the counter-spell will be inside the book, too."

"Can't you use your biblio-witchery to get it out?"

"That's not how it works," said Cass. "We can't use our magic on any old words. Just the ones from our specialist books. I suppose you don't have one, so you wouldn't know."

"Cass, stand there for a moment, dear," Aunt Candace interjected.

Cass looked up. "What for?"

Aunt Candace's hands glowed, as did the circle. We all braced ourselves, but the book stayed where it was. "No. If there was a deflector spell, it would have gone off."

Cass frowned. "The spell would have been aimed at where I'm standing."

"I thought it might knock some sense into you." Aunt Candace waved her hands over the circle. "Someone did a good job sealing this thing up. If it *does* have a soul trapped in it, it's under the magical equivalent of a steel cage."

"The dead man's soul is *inside* the book?" I asked.

"Where else would it be, floating around the library?" Cass rolled her eyes at me. "It's clever, really. The curse trapped the guy's soul in the book. Then the killer sealed the book so nobody can get it out."

"Which means it's staying here and not under Edwin's watch," said Aunt Candace. "I won't be made a fool of in my own library. I'll crack this."

"And if you get the book open, you'll find out who cast it?" The leather-bound pages looked too fragile to support a human soul,

"I have to undo the shields first," said Aunt Candace. "There are at least three layers on this thing. Curses are tricky to work at the best of times."

"Because they have to be cast with intention," Estelle said to me. "You have to really want to harm someone to use one, and each curse has different requirements. They're the most complex type of spell there is. Add in the fact that they put multiple layers of protection on the book itself, and it's most likely a witch or wizard who did it."

"A witch or wizard with unusual skill levels," added Aunt Candace. "Foolish, really. If they wanted the man dead, they could have used any old mundane method and yet they decided to use the showiest, most complex one possible."

"Then they wanted to make a statement," Cass said. "That, or their ego got in the way."

"And do you not think it's odd that they picked the library?" I asked. "I mean, they cursed one of our family's books. Is there anyone who'd be out to frame one of us for murder?"

Cass gave me a disdainful look. "Everyone in town uses the library. It's the best place to cast a curse and hide the body without inviting in too many questions. If it's someone with a grudge against our family, we'd have already dealt with them."

If you say so. "Aunt Candace, are you sure the curse was specifically aimed at Duncan?" I asked. "I mean, anyone could have picked it up."

"I wouldn't waste a curse this complex on a stranger," my aunt muttered. A pen and paper floated at her side, the pen writing by itself.

"What spell are you casting now?" I pointed at the paper.

"I'm not. I'm taking notes. This is going in my next space mystery novel."

Cass rolled her eyes. "Here we go again. Right, I'm done."

"You can't leave," Estelle said. "The police haven't removed the body."

"They're doing that now," said Aunt Adelaide from behind me. "Everyone, come back into the library."

We all moved, even Aunt Candace. Aunt Adelaide was the one in charge, after all.

Edwin stood next to the front desk, flanked by two huge brutish men in identical blue uniforms. They had grey skin and huge arms.

"Trolls," Estelle whispered. "Nice guys, actually. Just don't get on their bad side."

Aunt Candace halted behind us, her floating pen still scribbling away in her notepad. The trolls had covered Duncan's body, and another couple of uniformed people stood talking to the Reaper at the entrance. Aunt Adelaide strode towards them, while the rest of us hung back along with the rest of the crowd. The two elves exchanged whispered words. Tad lay in the hammock, his hat lopsided. And the vampire—

—was right behind me. I stiffened.

"Aurora Hawthorn," Dominic said.

Up close, he looked even more like a waxwork statue. His face was chalk white, his hair glossy black. His clothes were casual, but his way of standing echoed the other vampires I'd encountered. He sounded nothing like the men who'd come into the shop, but I found myself wanting to dive behind the nearest shelf.

"Relax," he said. "I mean you no harm. I simply wanted to introduce myself. I am Dominic."

"Uh. Hi." He extended a hand. It'd be rude not to shake it, so I did so, trying not to shudder. His hand was icy cold. About what I'd expect from a vampire, then.

Did he look like the sort of person who'd put a brutal curse on someone because he didn't like their poetry? Maybe.

"Not in the slightest," he said. "Personally, I find curses a crude method of dealing with one's enemies. I prefer a more direct approach."

"Er…" Did he mean biting people? "Sorry, I just found out about the mind-reading thing a few minutes ago."

If I was going to spend any more time around vampires, I'd need to work on controlling my thoughts.

"We can only read via eye contact usually," he commented. "And it's restricted to people within the same room. If that makes you feel more at ease."

"You can read minds," I said, inspiration striking. "Does that mean if the killer was in this room, you'd know who it was?"

He tilted his head. "Yes, unless the killer was adept at shielding their thoughts. It's possible."

"And they're not here? For definite?"

"No, but I wouldn't expect so," he said. "The book was in the victim's hands. That suggests the curse came on the instant he picked it up."

"So... the curse was already on the book before he picked it up, and the killer isn't in the library at all?"

"That would be the logical assumption," he said.

"Then the killer might have returned the book at any time, not today." I looked for Estelle. She and Cass stood by the stairs, in what appeared to be a whispered argument.

"That's also possible." His gaze went to the two trolls. "I don't think Edwin is going to get what he came here for."

Hmm. He thought the killer wasn't here. Then again, it wasn't like I knew for sure what *he* was thinking.

"I heard you were at the last poetry night," I said. "Er, with a group of vampires." Wait, what was I doing? I had no business questioning anyone. He'd already talked to the police, besides.

"Oh, that," he said. "I wasn't here for the poetry night. A group of my colleagues and I were invited by your aunt to make corrections to certain historical books, and we witnessed that abomination of a poetry reading. My friends were a little too direct about expressing their disdain."

"And how did Duncan react?" I asked.

"He didn't seem bothered," said Dominic. "He remained cheerfully oblivious to his lack of talent until the end. I can see the advantages of not having the ability to read minds in that particular case."

Hmm. "So you said my aunt invited you to correct the history books? Why?"

"Vampires live long lives," he said. "And I work in the local university's history department, so it's important that I fact-check all the books for my students. All the centuries blur together in the memory, so I occasionally need a refresher."

"Uh—how old are you?"

"Old enough." Another flash of fangs. *Ah, forget I asked.* What was I doing, making casual conversation with a vampire?

"Give it time and this will be far from the strangest thing you've done, Aurora."

I took a step back. "Can you not eavesdrop on my thoughts?"

"You're fairly transparent. I apologise."

Of course I'm transparent if you're in my head. Maybe it wasn't his fault that he could find out everyone's secrets at any given time, but it was still creepy.

He flashed me a smile. "Maybe you'll change your mind."

Maybe hell would freeze over first. I managed a grimace. "I'm still getting used to the paranormal thing."

"Naturally," said the Reaper. Once again, I hadn't seen him cross the room, let alone sneak up behind me.

"How did you move so quietly?" I asked.

"Trade secret." He gave me a smile, too, thankfully fang-free. If anything, it made him look positively angelic... for the angel of death. "Did your aunt manage to get anything from the book?"

"She can't get it open," I said. "There's some sort of shield spell on it. So you can't get Duncan's soul until the book's opened?"

"Not until the curse is removed." He pushed back his blond

curls with one hand, and I noted that he'd strapped the scythe to his back again. "I'm leaving now, but I might come back later to have another look around. I'll see you soon, Aurora."

Coming from the Grim Reaper? Not exactly reassuring.

The vampire laughed under his breath. I gave him a warning look and went to join Estelle, who stood talking to Aunt Candace—given Cass's absence, she must have failed to convince her to stick around.

"They'll be back," said Aunt Candace, jerking her head at the police trolls' retreating backs. "I still can't get a handle on the bloody book. Stubborn thing."

"So you don't know who might have cursed it?" I asked. "Dominic—the vampire—he said that since he can read minds, he might have been able to identify the killer. But he didn't pick up anything from the people in the room."

"That means nothing," Aunt Candace said. "Some people are more adept at shielding their thoughts than others."

Yet another thing I needed to work on, apparently. "Well, if someone else is the killer, they could have cursed the book *before* returning it to the library, right?"

"You're right," Estelle said, slapping a palm to her forehead. "I should have thought of that. If the curse was put on the book beforehand, it didn't take place in the library at all. That's why nobody saw it."

"That means it might not have been directed at Duncan," I said.

Estelle shook her head. "A malicious curse like that... the odds of the killer making sure it reached its target are high."

"Or they didn't care who else got caught in the process," said Aunt Candace. "Hmm. It has so many possibilities. I'm trying to decide—should I make it a cursed piece of space junk or a lost artefact my characters find on an alien planet?"

"How about neither?" Aunt Adelaide strode over to us. I looked past her and saw the police had gone, taking

Duncan's body with them. "The best thing to do at this stage is to reopen the doors and carry on as usual. Where's Cass?"

"Here," said Cass, appearing with Sylvester hovering at her side. "You're seriously going to move on as though nothing happened?"

Aunt Adelaide blew out a breath. "I know it's been a rough couple of hours, but I highly doubt Fiona will cancel her classes. That means we need to have the classrooms set up and ready. There's a group of business wizards from out of town coming this afternoon, too—I'll handle that one."

"I'll keep working on undoing the curse on the book," Aunt Candace said.

"And I'll help," said Cass, but Aunt Adelaide caught her arm. "Not so fast. The book only needs one of you, and I'm intending to conduct a thorough sweep of the ground floor in case any more curses are lingering around. That means you'll run the front desk."

"That's not fair," she spat. "Aunt Candace will just sneak off to work on her manuscript when she thinks nobody's looking."

From Aunt Candace's guilty expression, that was exactly what she'd planned on doing.

"Can't Estelle do it?" Cass added.

"Estelle has volunteered to go through the records to find who checked out that book," said Aunt Adelaide. "She'll give Rory a rundown of the system, too. Sylvester, do make sure Cass stay put."

"With pleasure," said the owl.

Leaving a grumbling Cass behind, Estelle and I went to the section of shelves behind the front desk. They contained pile upon pile of dusty record books showing every book that had been removed and returned in the last few decades.

"The curse was almost certainly put on the book by the last person who checked it out," Estelle said as we walked.

"Unless someone else did it here in the library, of course, but as I said, we'd have noticed. What *did* Cass do with that record book? It's supposed to be at the front desk... ah, there it is." She reached a reading nook, where a large bound book lay underneath two books with spaceships on the covers. She pulled out the bound book and left the other titles.

"Are those Aunt Candace's?" I guessed.

"Oh, feel free to borrow them. Just don't tell her you're reading them, it freaks her out."

I picked up the two sci-fi titles, while Estelle carried the record book to a nearby desk and opened it.

"The curse might have been cast at any time, but we'll know which dates it was removed from the library." She turned the page. "Deadly curses don't always lose their potency with time. Usually, we don't deal with the deadly type. More like the 'turn your enemy into a toad' or 'make their hair fall out' type. The curse on that book is an advanced one."

"And the killer sealed it shut," I added. "Was that a curse, or a spell?"

"Spell," she said. "Curses are typically directed at a person. Spells can be used on anything. You'll learn more about the classifications when you begin your training properly."

I turned this over in my head. The number of things I didn't know seemed as endless as the books on the shelves.

"There," she said, running her finger down the page. "The book was returned yesterday. The last person to take it out was... Alice from the familiar shop. Odd. I didn't think she dealt with curses."

"She wasn't here for the questioning?" I asked.

"No. I'll ask Mum if we can speak to her. Though she wasn't kidding when she said a lot of people are coming in today."

"Even after the murder?" I asked. "Or hasn't word spread by now?"

"It will." Her mouth pinched. "But we might get a few hours of normality, provided none of us is hauled off for questioning again."

An almighty boom shook the shelves.

"Or maybe not," she said.

The two of us sprinted out of the archives to the front desk. I stared in alarm at the smoke pouring out of the half-open door to the room containing Aunt Candace and the cursed book, but the other patrons hadn't even looked in that direction. Nor had Cass moved from her post at the front desk.

"Aren't you worried about your aunt?" I asked her.

Cass shrugged. "If she blows herself up, guess who gets her royalties?"

So much for family love.

Estelle and I hurried through the Reading Corner and found Aunt Candace in the empty classroom, waving her wand to dispel a thick cloud of smoke. Her eyebrows were gone, her hair was even wilder than usual, and the book remained where it was, floating within the circle. The smell of burning filled the room.

"The book is cursed," she announced.

"You don't say?" Estelle said. "What did you do this time, try to blow the covers off?"

"Excuse me?" a loud voice intervened. It was Samson of the ever-accumulating late fees. "Can you keep it down?"

"My aunt nearly blew herself up," I told him.

"Yes, I know. I have an exam to study for." He scowled at the floating book. "I thought you were running a library, not a laboratory."

"Samson," Estelle said. "If you wish to use one of the quiet rooms, there are plenty available. And have you returned those books yet?"

A pause. "No." He sloped off back to the Reading Corner.

"Sorry," she said. "He's not our biggest fan. He and Cass get into fights at least once a week."

"Why does he come here if he doesn't like our family?"

"Because we're the best library in town," Aunt Candace said.

"You mean the only library in town." Sylvester flew over our heads and sniffed at the spell circle. "Next time you might want to try shielding."

"I did," said my now eyebrow-less aunt. "I think the book might have a defence mechanism on it."

"I can't imagine what might have given you that idea," said Sylvester blandly.

With a wave of her wand, Aunt Candace's eyebrows were restored. "Blasted book. It's safe to say it's immune to most regular spells."

"Any luck?" asked Aunt Adelaide, appearing behind us.

"There you are, Mum," said Estelle. "Rory and I have found out who last checked out the book—Alice. You know, from the familiar shop. Can we head over and speak to her now, or do you need us to help handle things here?"

"Oh, go ahead," said Aunt Adelaide. "Try to be back within the hour, though—I need some assistance preparing the conference room."

"I'll come and take care of it," said Aunt Candace, with a disgruntled look at the floating book.

"I'll hound her until she does," Sylvester said.

Estelle, meanwhile, led the way back through the library and outside into the bustling square. Today, there were plenty of people walking around. I'd been too overwhelmed to take it all in yesterday, but now I spotted a bakery, a flower shop, a bank. The library occupied the central spot, taking up an entire side of the square, and you couldn't help but look in its direction as you passed by.

"There it is." Estelle led the way to a small red-brick shop at the northwest corner of the square. "Alice owns the town's only familiar shop. I can't think why she'd have wanted a book of curses, though."

She pushed open the red-painted door, and we entered the small shop.

Spacious cages lined the walls. Birds flew freely, nesting in the beams criss-crossing the ceiling. Cats of all shades and sizes napped in the cages or prowled around the floors. Brightly-coloured fish filled tanks along one wall, while cages containing rabbits and odd-looking rodents occupied the other. A riot of sound filled the small shop, squawks and purrs and growls.

I ducked when a little black bird swooped dangerously close to my head.

"Jet!" said a stern voice.

A curvaceous young woman popped out from behind a shelf. What appeared to be a furry snake coiled around her neck, its head peering between strands of dark curly hair.

"Hey there, Estelle," she said, eyeing me with interest. "You're new."

"Rory's my cousin," Estelle said. "She just moved here."

She beamed. "Hey, Rory. I'm Alice."

"Nice to meet you," I said.

"We're in a bit of a situation at the moment," said Estelle. "I don't know if you heard yet, but Duncan was murdered this morning. He died at the library."

"Really?" Her face fell, and a chorus of shrieks broke out from among the cages.

"Can the animals understand us?" I couldn't help asking.

"Some of them," she said. "He's dead?"

"He was cursed," Estelle said. "Specifically, by one of our

books. Our records said you were the last person to take out the *Advanced Book of Curses*, so I wondered if you knew anything. You returned it yesterday?"

"I did." Her expression shadowed. "Someone used a curse from the book?"

"Someone put a curse *on* the book," said Estelle. "You had the book for a week. Did you loan it to anyone else it during that time?"

"I did," she said. "I had to deal with a situation with one of the animals. Turns out it was a spell and not a curse, so I didn't need the book, and... well, I handed it over to the curse-breaker to help with a client. As usual, he wouldn't say what he needed it for."

"Oh," said Estelle. "Mr Bennet, right?"

She nodded. "Sorry that happened. I didn't know Duncan well, but he seemed like a decent guy. I hope they catch whoever did it."

She sounded sincere, and certainly didn't look like the type of person who'd curse someone to death. I'd pick the vampire as a more likely suspect than her. Not that I could always trust in appearances when it came to all things magical, as I'd learned already.

The little black bird flew low over my head again, making me cringe. The bird cawed, and Estelle flapped a hand at it. "Shoo."

The bird cawed back—and landed on my shoulder.

I froze. The little black bird sat there, beady eyes fixed on me. His beak looked sharp, but his glossy feathers and round eyes weren't threatening in the slightest.

"Er..." Estelle looked perplexed. "I think it wants to be friends with you."

I twisted my head to look at the bird. It was hard to be scared of a creature small enough to fit into my palm. "Is it a raven or a crow?"

"Jet is a crow," said Alice, her face lighting up. "Interesting."

"What's interesting?" I asked.

Estelle smiled. "I think he wants to be your familiar."

"Caw," said the crow.

I blinked. "A crow can be a familiar?"

"Any animal can," said Estelle. "Cats are the most popular."

"Yes." Alice smiled. "But we have a lot of variety. If you want to take him, there's a fee, but it's discounted for a familiar arrangement. I can use a couple of spells to check if you like."

"I…" Had no idea what to say. "I haven't got paid yet…"

"I'll handle it," Estelle said. "Familiars are great to have, especially if you're new to magic."

"I don't know about this. Birds and I aren't exactly—"

The crow cawed again, climbing around the back of my neck to my other shoulder. I tensed, then gave a nervous laugh when his feathers tickled me.

"He does like you." Alice clapped her hands and the crow swooped over to her.

"Can he understand us?" I asked.

"Yes," said Estelle. "You'll be able to communicate in a way —not with words, but most witches share a close bond with their familiar and have an innate understanding of one another."

If I had to pick an animal to share a common understanding with, a bird would be bottom of the list. Okay, maybe one step above sharks and alligators. The little bird sat on Alice's hand, while she waved her wand at him.

"Yes, you have the familiar bond, all right," she said, pocketing her wand with a satisfied smile. "I'm sure it'll strengthen with time. Birds are self-sufficient as far as familiars go. Don't worry about paying now—I'll send the bill through to the library."

Jet cawed again and flew over to land on my arm. A familiar. *My* familiar. The magical world wasn't out of surprises yet.

7

I left the shop along with my unexpected companion, who rode on my shoulder as though he was having the time of his life.

"What'll your mum say about this?" I asked Estelle. "I mean, I know you already have an owl in the library, but wouldn't she want us to tell her before bringing him in?"

"No, Cass has had all kinds of weird pets. If you ask me, she has one right now, that's why she kept disappearing this morning."

I looked away from the bird. "How'd you figure that one out?"

"She split up with her boyfriend over the weekend," she said. "That means she'll swear off guys for the foreseeable future, and she doesn't invite other people into her favourite section of the library. Therefore, an animal. I just hope it isn't a dangerous one this time."

"This time?" I said.

"Cass has... interesting hobbies," she said.

No kidding. "And will Sylvester object?"

"I wouldn't say he'd be thrilled, but it's rare for a family to share a familiar, and you *are* new, so it makes sense that another animal might pick you."

The crow took flight and soared close above my head, and I resisted the impulse to wince when his claw caught my hair. I was living in a magical library with flying books and an owl—a crow should be no trouble to adjust to. Besides, it would be nice to have a winged companion who didn't laugh at me when I fell through the stairs or make sarcastic comments about my lack of magical talent.

"You can tell him to fly ahead to the library," she said. "He's smart, he'll figure it out."

"Sure." I looked up at the little bird. "I live at the library. If you fly back there, I can meet you. Er, and watch out for the owl."

Jet chirped, then flew in the direction of the library. Sorted. At least until I had to explain myself to my aunts later, anyway. I adjusted my grip on the bag and found a business card inside it, along with a handful of free vouchers for what looked like every shop or business in town.

"Wow, is Alice this nice to all the newbies?" I asked.

"Only the pretty ones."

"I'd introduce her to my friend Laney if I was allowed to bring her here. Also, I have enough free muffin vouchers for a week."

"Oh, cool. Duncan used to work as an assistant at the bakery." She indicated a large, bright shop across from us. "I'd normally pop in there to grab a muffin, but there's a chance Edwin and the police might be questioning his co-workers."

I peered through the glass but didn't any elves, just a mouth-watering display of tarts, pies and pastries.

Estelle saw me looking. "Hmm. I suppose we could pay a visit, since you have all those vouchers. I'll grab some flowers from Harold's first."

She ducked into the flower shop on our right, which was staffed by a short man with a whiskery moustache.

"He's a wererabbit," she said in an undertone, before ordering a bouquet of flowers. The two of them chatted amicably. Estelle seemed to know everyone in the town we'd met so far. Perks of working at the library, I guessed.

The bakery was a bright, cheerful place filled with delicious smells, but the curvy black woman behind the counter wore a frown and her eyes were red. Given the number of flowers and cards behind the desk, we weren't the first to visit today.

"Hey, Zee," said Estelle, walking over to her with the flowers. "I'm sorry about Duncan."

She sniffed. "You found him, right? I just don't understand it."

"Nor me," Estelle waved her wand, and the flowers arranged themselves in a jar on the counter. "Can we use these vouchers and get a selection of those muffins?"

"Sure." The woman waved her wand and levitated several of the muffins into a bag. "Here you go. Sorry about the state of the place... I guess I'll be looking for a new assistant." She blinked, noticing me for the first time. "Oh. You're new."

"I'm Rory. Estelle's cousin."

"Oh, the lost cousin?"

"I don't know about lost, but I am new in town. I moved here yesterday."

"And you're working at the library? I suppose I don't need to ask." She tried a smile that didn't reach her eyes. "Wonderful place. No wonder Duncan was there all the time."

"He was?" I asked.

"Well, yeah, he was a student," she said. "Not that he ever did much studying. I think he only went there to write that poetry of his. He talked about it all the time. Said he was going to win awards."

Neither Estelle nor I knew what to say to that. By all accounts, his poetry had been awful.

She let out a heavy sigh. "Sorry for being morose."

"Oh, don't apologise," said Estelle. "Take care of yourself, okay?"

We left the shop, and Estelle opened the bag of muffins. "There's sweet or savoury. Take your pick," she said.

"Er… I'll go with sweet."

She passed me the muffin. I turned it over in my hand and took a bite. My taste buds exploded with the flavour of some sort of wild berries. "Oh, wow."

"Isn't it divine?" said Estelle. "That's Zee's work. Her witchy talent is for baking."

"I can see that." I chewed, savouring every mouthful. "Was Duncan's talent the same?"

"No, he only worked there as a part-time thing," said Estelle. "To supplement his student loan, I'd guess."

I grimaced. "Of all the ideas to copy from the normal world, why student loans? Can't they just magic the debt away?"

She laughed. "If only."

I took another bite. "I might be back there tomorrow. I have enough vouchers."

"I don't blame you." She chewed on her mouthful. "I don't know if Zee will look for another assistant yet. The one downside to our isolated communities is that it's often hard to find specialists like her. But that's part of what makes our town unique, aside from the library. We get thousands of tourists in summer."

"I can imagine," I said. "What was that she said about me being the lost cousin?"

"Ah," said Estelle. "I forgot, but it's nothing bad, don't worry."

"Oh?" I said.

"It's Aunt Candace's fault," said Estelle. "One of her books is… sort of based on your dad's life story. With permission, of course. It's the only book she published under her own name, so the whole town has read it by now."

I swallowed a mouthful of muffin, coughing. "Seriously?"

"She writes across genres, and your father's epic romance with your mother inspired that particular tale. She changed the names and details, but the book was dedicated… well, to you. The lost cousin."

Wow. I didn't know what to say. "I guess that's kind of flattering. Not sure I want to read about my parents' epic love affair…"

"It's actually pretty good," she said. "She usually warns us before she steals things from our family drama, but Cass has blown up at her a few times over her use of her old boyfriends as villains."

I grinned. "I bet. So is that sort of story popular? I mean, my parents' love story?"

"Oh, there's a whole section in our Romance area of "Paranormal and Normal romances". Star-crossed lovers are very popular," she said. "Same in the normal world, right?"

The lost cousin. I still felt lost in a lot of ways, especially when we left the square down an unfamiliar street alongside the clock tower and made our way to the seafront. The tide was in, and I spotted the pier she'd mentioned further down on our right. It didn't appear to have anything on it, like the rides on Blackpool's piers, but the bitterly cold wind put me off the idea of visiting the beach today.

Estelle and I finished our muffins on the short walk to the curse-breaker's shop. It was about the same size as the familiar shop but was almost empty and smelled of burning and something sharp and unpleasant. The same smell that'd filled the air when Aunt Candace had been trying to undo the spell on the book.

The man behind the counter, presumably Mr Bennet, was tall and thin with a sour face.

"Yes?" he asked. "Need me to remove a curse?"

"Actually… we might," said Estelle, with a glance at me. "Someone put a deadly curse on the copy of *The Advanced Book of Curses* from our library, which caused the death of a patron."

"Is that so? I'm sorry to hear it." He didn't sound very sorry at all.

"Alice told us she loaned you the book when she had it out of the library," Estelle went on. "Last week, in fact."

Mr Bennet's lips pursed. "Yes, I looked at the book. I do occasionally need to consult another source if I run into a particularly tricky curse to break."

"And what curse was this?" I asked.

"Customer confidentiality." His tone was flat.

"You're aware the police will probably come to question you, right?" Estelle said, her mouth thinning.

"If Edwin wants to know, then that's different," he said.

"This is a man's life we're talking about, though," said Estelle. "He was killed by a soul-stealing curse. Have you ever heard of those?"

His expression darkened. "Very dark magic, stealing a soul. I'm afraid I can't help you. Your family is more versed in dark magic than I am."

"We certainly aren't," said Estelle, her friendly manner vanishing. "How would one go about removing a curse from *inside* an object? The book appears to have been put under a series of protective spells."

"That," he said, "would require a spell-breaker, not a curse-breaker. Good day."

Estelle's eyes narrowed, and she turned her back, leaving the shop.

"That was nice," I said to her. "Dark magic?"

"He knew Grandma," explained Estelle. "Let's just say they disagreed on their approaches to magic. That's what my mum said, anyway. The library isn't made of dark magic. It's nonsense."

"Even Cass?" I was only half joking. Though for all her attempts to make me feel unwelcome, she'd never used a hostile spell against me. Unless she'd been the one moving the stairs, that is.

"Speaking of Cass, she'll be hopping mad that we've been gone for too long. We should head back."

After a last look at the sea, I turned away, the cold breeze buffeting us all the way past the clock tower to the town square.

"Why not tell him about Aunt Candace not being able to remove the curse?" I asked.

"You might have noticed, but he's not a fan of bibliowitches," she said. "Also, I don't doubt the police will end up questioning him eventually, and Edwin won't be happy if we hand the book to a potential suspect."

"Makes sense," I said. "Except if he can undo the curse…"

"If Aunt Candace can't, then he definitely won't be able to," she said. "Curses might be his area of expertise, but books are *our* area. Cursed ones included."

And that was that. Nothing to do but go back to the library. With any luck, the police would show up at Mr Bennet's shop and he'd be forced to reveal who his secret client was.

As we neared the library, my gaze snagged on the roof. The place was tall enough that it wasn't immediately obvious, but I could swear there was a whole extra floor above the main library.

"Oh, don't ask questions like that," said Estelle when I mentioned this. "Especially to Aunt Candace. I think she put some of the corridors in there herself, but the real culprit is

Grandma. If you find anything weird, chances are, it has her fingerprints all over it."

"Is anything here *not* weird?"

She grinned. "Point taken. I have to say, I've missed having someone new to hang out with. Don't get me wrong, we have people in and out of the place all the time, but it's not the same. Being a biblio-witch sets us apart in a lot of ways. We're different."

"Different isn't a bad thing." It didn't seem to hurt Estelle, anyway. She seemed sociable and popular and had lots of friends. I'd been pretty bad at maintaining friendships in adulthood. I'd had Laney and some others from school, but most of my classmates had moved to the big cities to find work after graduating from university, or travelled the world, or started families. I'd stayed put, for the sake of the bookshop.

A pang hit me. Already I was starting to forget that life. I had no doubt Abe would do his best to keep the bookshop running, but guilt soured my mood, and I walked into the library with my head down.

Without warning, a book shot over my head, its pages clipping my scalp. Samson faced off against Cass, his straw-like hair askew and a scowl on his face. Both of them had their wands out. Cass waved hers and several books lifted into the air, throwing themselves at Samson.

Samson waved his own wand, and the books flew to the side, only to change direction as though they had a mind of their own. As they flew overhead, Estelle grabbed my arm, pulling me out of the line of fire. The books spun around, pages spread like wings, and one of them hit Samson square in the face.

"Cass!" Estelle said. "That's enough! If you damage the books, you'll be the one paying fees to the library for the next decade."

Samson pushed himself upright. His nose was bleeding. I took an uncertain step toward him. "Are you okay?"

"Don't touch me," he spat. With a last furious look around the library, he stormed out of the doors.

Cass marched after him, wielding her black-covered book. She tapped a word with her hand, and I heard Samson's furious swearing outside the door.

"Just sending him a goodbye message." Her mouth twisted. "Lazy sod. He returned *one* book, and it had writing in the margins. He said he didn't do it, but it's a blatant lie."

"You didn't need to wreck the place," Estelle said, picking up one of the books she'd thrown at him.

"I said if he wanted the books so badly, he could catch them," she said. "Aunt Adelaide is way too lenient on him."

"What kicked things off this time?" Estelle asked. "Come on, he does the same thing every week. You don't normally try to burn out your magic and damage the books."

Cass spoke through gritted teeth. "It might have escaped your attention, but thanks to whoever left Duncan's body in here, we're behind on everything and I'm wasting my time listening to losers like him making pathetic excuses for defiling our property."

Estelle picked up one of the books. "Well, you didn't have to terrify the other patrons."

"It's your fault for clearing off," she said. "Did you take Aurora to *every* shop in town?"

"It's been less than an hour," Estelle said. "I brought you a muffin, but if you're going to be a pedant, I'll eat it myself."

The crow chose that moment to land on my shoulder, fluffing his feathers.

"Why is there a crow in here?" Cass asked.

"He's my familiar," I said.

Cass snorted. "Is he now."

"What's so funny?" I asked. "It's not so unusual for a witch to have a familiar." Maybe it was unusual for someone who didn't like birds to have one as a familiar, but I didn't make the rules.

"Sylvester is going to be thrilled."

Estelle handed her the bag from the bakery. Cass accepted the peace offering, while the other patrons stopped gawking in the hope that she and Samson would resume their fight and returned to their reading corners.

Aunt Adelaide came out of the archives. "Got it out of her system, has she?"

"You knew?" I asked.

"Yes, I did. Samson deserved it, to tell you the truth. We don't have many rules here, but it's bad manners to defile the books."

"He said he didn't do it," said Estelle, with an eye-roll. "Anyway, I got you a muffin. We detoured via Zee's bakery."

"Oh, how is she coping?" she asked. "I might pop by later... it's such a shame."

"We're already behind," Cass said snippily. "If Estelle and Rory hadn't spent the morning eating muffins and buying familiars, they might have lent a helping hand."

"We also learned that the curse-breaker might have been the last person to see the cursed book before it was returned to the library," I said, "but he won't tell us what he was using it for."

Cass bit into the muffin. "And that's relevant... how?"

"Because someone died in here a few hours ago?" I turned to Aunt Adelaide. "Is there anything you need us to do?"

"Yes," said Aunt Adelaide. "Your aunt's disappeared. Can you two find her for me?"

"Isn't she working on the cursed book?" Estelle moved around the desk, and I followed her. Dropping her voice, she added, "I don't blame her for hiding, considering Cass was in charge. I can't wait until the next guy comes along. She's only bearable to be around if she's in a relationship."

"I'd feel bad for the guy," I said. "Maybe she and the Late Returns Guy are in some hate-to-love thing."

Estelle cracked up laughing. "I bet Aunt Candace could write one hell of a book out of it."

"Has she ever written Cass into one of her books?"

"Yes, but she doesn't read them," said Aunt Candace from behind a nearby shelf. "Says they're not her thing."

Estelle turned to her. "Rory found out about the lost cousin dedication. Told you it was a bad idea."

Aunt Candace shrugged. "Roger didn't mind. He said he was a fan of the story, actually."

"Your dad used to read romance books?" Estelle asked.

"Pretty sure there wasn't any type of book he didn't read," I said. "But—wait, does that mean your books are for sale in the normal world as well as this one?"

"Obviously," said Aunt Candace. "They're dressed up as fiction. Nobody questions it. Why would they?"

"Fair point," I said. "Do you sell more to normals than paranormals? Or both?"

"Both," said Estelle. "The paranormal world loves her. Half the town would lose their minds if they found out she lived right here."

Aunt Candace shuddered. "No. I'd never get any peace then."

"Your last fantasy caper was on the best-seller list for three weeks," Estelle said. "Everyone in the paranormal world was raving about it."

Aunt Candace backed away. "Don't say things like that, it interferes with my concentration. And if your mother's looking for me, tell her I'm looking for high-level spell-breaking spells. Whatever's on that cursed book is immune to everything I've tried."

"The curse-breaker suggested hiring a spell-breaker," Estelle said. "The weird thing is, though—he had the book himself a few days ago. Borrowed it from Alice to help with a client, and he wouldn't tell us who it was."

"He wouldn't?" Aunt Candace frowned. "Usually he deals with simpler curses. Hair loss, raining frogs, that type of thing. Not the type of curse where people lose their souls."

"Is losing his soul the same as dying, then?" I asked. "How does that work?"

"Best ask the Reaper that, not me," Aunt Candace said.

Yeah, I don't think so.

———

The rest of the day passed quickly. Estelle and I helped customers find books in the library's most popular areas, giving me the chance to learn the ground floor better. I tried to rein in my questions about the various locked doors and oddities scattered among the shelves, but I suspected it'd take a lifetime to unravel all the library's secrets.

After the library closed up for the night, I returned to my room to find my newly acquired crow familiar sitting on the bed. "Oh, there you are," I said. "I wondered where you'd gone. I haven't told my aunts about you yet..."

Aunt Adelaide had spent the day running around dealing with the patrons' various demands or sending Estelle or me to deal with them. Cass had pulled another disappearing act after her stint at the front desk, while Aunt Candace had made one last valiant attempt to crack open the cursed book and caused all the lights to turn off instead.

The crow fluffed his feathers. According to the familiar guidebook Alice had given me, he couldn't actually talk to me, but we were supposed to innately understand one another.

"You want to come and meet the family?" I asked. "I'm guessing you've probably run—or flown—into Sylvester."

Cass seemed to be the owl's favourite. Then again, I'd been with Estelle most of the time, so I'd had minimal opportunities to fall through missing steps or floors.

Jet hopped onto my shoulder. "You're sure you want to be my familiar?"

The crow made a chirping noise.

"At least you found my room," I went on. "The library's probably less confusing to navigate when you have wings, but I'll give you the tour on the way down to dinner."

To my relief, the corridor looked the way it was supposed to when I left my room with Jet perched on my shoulder. I took Jet with me to the ground floor of the library and pointed out all the areas I'd learned about today.

"And that's the Reading Corner—"

"Who in the world are you talking to?" Cass asked from behind me.

Jet peered curiously at Cass, then flew over to her. She caught the crow on her outstretched hand. "Oh. It's your familiar."

"I guess he likes you," I said, feeling inexplicably annoyed that he'd approached her so readily. Maybe he just liked people in general and hadn't singled me out after all.

"All animals like me," Cass said, lifting her hand to look more closely at the crow. "He's a little small for a familiar. What skills has he demonstrated?"

"Er..." I was stumped. "He seems intelligent."

"More than you? That's not saying a lot."

"Cass," Estelle said, climbing downstairs behind me. Jet's head snapped up at the new arrival and he flew over to her, landing on her shoulder.

"See, he likes everyone," I said, taking the lead and going into the dining room. Aunt Adelaide was in the process of levitating plates onto the table, while Aunt Candace sat at the far end, scribbling into a notebook.

Jet took flight again and landed on Aunt Candace's scribbling hand. She jumped violently, scribbling across the page, and swore.

"So that's your familiar?" Aunt Adelaide finished lowering the plates onto the table and gave him a once-over. "I wouldn't have thought a bird would be your style, Rory. Not that I'd claim to be an expert, but the majority of witches and wizards bond with a cat."

"Birds and I don't usually get along, but Alice said he picked me." I sat down, and Estelle took the seat on my other side. "So how does the familiar thing work? He seems to like everyone, not just me."

"There are some spells which can only be cast with the aid of a familiar." Aunt Adelaide said. "Sylvester is different, since he belongs to the family. Some witches find their familiars match their personalities, others find they're polar opposites. You'll get to know one another in time."

Jet hopped on the table beside me. "Alice said he'd be self-sufficient. Am I supposed to feed him?"

"Oh, he'll have found his way into the Magical Creatures Division by now." Aunt Adelaide finished laying out the plates and took a seat beside Aunt Candace. "Besides, I leave food out for the birds all the time. Just as long as he doesn't get into a fight with Sylvester."

"I don't think he's the fighting type," I said.

"You have one thing in common, then." Cass sat down at the far end of the table and picked up her fork. "Except for the lack of style."

"Cass, are you incapable of opening your mouth without an insult coming out of it?" Estelle said.

"No," Cass said, shovelling potatoes into her mouth.

"Pretty sure there's a cure for that in one of the books

here." I started eating. Aunt Adelaide, as it turned out, was an amazing cook. I'd have a hard time picking between her cooking and Zee's homemade muffins.

Aunt Candace gave a laugh. "This is going to be interesting."

I spotted the pen and notebook floating at her side. "Are you recording our conversation?"

"I have to get my research somewhere, don't I?"

"I have news," interrupted Aunt Adelaide. "Elliot heard about Rory and has insisted on inviting himself round for dinner tomorrow. Cass and Estelle's father," she added, for my benefit. "We divorced a decade ago, but he's still a good friend of the family."

Cass made a disparaging noise.

"Dad's fine," said Estelle. "I wondered if he'd volunteer himself as your magic tutor, Rory… you'll need one. A tutor for regular magic, not for biblio-witchery."

"Yeah, no chance of *that*," said Cass. "He's not the first person who hoped he'd tame the library by marrying one of us. But I thought you had a date tomorrow, Mum. Blowing it off for him?"

Aunt Adelaide went brick red. "Really, Cass. No, we rescheduled. Until this murder business is taken care of."

"Not another policeman?" Cass said.

Aunt Adelaide scowled. "Please refrain from commenting on my love life at the table. Unless you'd like me to comment on yours."

Aunt Candace's notebook practically vibrated with excitement. I could tell this was a frequent argument.

"When do my magic lessons start?" I asked, trying to change the subject.

Aunt Adelaide turned to me. "Tomorrow, we'll see about you starting you off in magical theory. The current law states that you have to pass the first exam of the entry-level class before you can apply for a wand. As for biblio-witchery, I'll arrange for the library to provide you with your own pen, notebook, and Biblio-Witch Inventory. For now, we'll stick to teaching you the basics of the library."

I grinned. I had a familiar, and before long, I'd get to learn magic for real. Whatever Cass said, I wasn't going anywhere.

8

_____

The next morning, I woke to a bird shrieking in my ear.

"It's time for your first magic lesson!" proclaimed Sylvester, perching on the end of my bed.

"No need to shout." I looked blearily around. Jet was nowhere in sight. No wonder. "What kind of magic lesson are we talking about?"

"A non-existent one at the rate you're going. Don't get too excited. You won't get a proper book or wand until you can prove you're not incompetent."

"Hey, I used magic once already." I rubbed the sleep from my eyes. "How do you know I'll be that bad at it?"

"Because your familiar is a crow," he said. "Not a very bright one, either."

"Better a crow than a—"

The owl's wings spread wide, making him look three times his usual size. "Might want to rethink before you finish that sentence."

"I need more coffee before I can think." I pushed the bedcovers aside. "Shoo. Let me get dressed in peace."

"I'm concerned you won't know which way to put your shirt on, the state you're in." He took flight, swooping around the room.

I swatted at him. "I don't need an owl as a nanny. Maybe I'll mark this room as an owl-free zone."

"You can't do that, dear. The library makes the rules."

Luckily, he didn't hang around to berate me while I pulled on my clothes, wishing I could grab a coffee to go. I made a mental note to get a kettle for my room for the days where the library wouldn't let me walk downstairs in a straight line. I'd need it.

Shockingly, I got lost on the way downstairs. The third time I walked to the corridor's end looking for the stairs, the floor opened up in front of me, revealing a slide. A slide was better than a missing stair, so I shrugged and climbed into it.

A mistake. I slid halfway down, then got stuck. That's what I got for making decisions while half-asleep. I shuffled down a few inches, mourning my dignity. At least nobody could see me in here.

Sylvester's laughter echoed down the slide behind me. *Or maybe not.*

The owl's voice came from behind my shoulder. "Want me to fly you out?"

"Can you do that?"

"No." He snorted. "Well done. You'll have to wait for someone to pull you out. Or send a smoke signal."

"Hilarious." It was lucky I wasn't claustrophobic. "Can't you fly to my aunt and tell her?"

"She won't get you out either. You know you're sitting in the garbage chute, don't you?"

"What?"

"Joking, joking."

"You!" I twisted around to give him a glare and hit my head on the ceiling. Ow.

The owl laughed again, the sound growing fainter by the second as he flew away. Wonderful.

I swore, shuffled forwards a few more metres, then abruptly dropped out of the slide into a ball pit.

"The library sent you to the kiddies' play area." Sylvester flew over my head. "Probably because the average age for a new witch is five years old. Ha."

"If you tell Cass, I'll yank out your tail feathers."

"You would never." He gave an indignant squawk and flew off, while I picked my way out of the ball pit, now thoroughly wide awake. I'd had entirely too much humiliation for this hour in the morning.

I walked out of the kids' play area and got my bearings. At least I'd landed on the right floor. I assumed my lesson would take place in one of the classrooms, so I made my way past the Reading Corner. Spotting an open door, I found Aunt Candace inside.

"Ah, Rory," she said, beckoning me in. "My sister has designated me as your theory tutor until you pass your wand exam. I'll not waste time pretending to be a halfway decent teacher, so let's get that part out of the way to avoid disappointment later down the line."

"Er, okay." I entered and took a seat in the front row. A pen and notepad lay on my desk beside a textbook open to the first double page spread, titled, "Basic Definitions".

"Your task is to read and copy the main points from the chapter," Aunt Candace said in a bored voice. "Every type of magic has a definition. The academy states you have to match their exact wording without any deviation. As long as you refrain from demonstrating any ingenuity, you should be fine."

Someone had strong feelings on the magical education system, apparently.

"All right..." I turned to the page. "This is about the different types of magic, right?"

"Yes, it is," said Aunt Candace. "I find it limiting, but they do like their traditions."

I read over the definitions. Spells, curses and hexes were all different. Hexes were hostile spells cast on a person with a wand, while curses could be put on an object instead of a person or set on a timer to hit their intended target a week after the caster actually used the curse.

No wonder the town needed a professional curse-breaker to sort out the aftermath. But nothing in the beginner's book said anything about curses removing people's souls. Not really a surprise, since the cursed book had stumped even my aunts.

I spent an hour copying out the various definitions, then Aunt Candace dismissed me. I found Estelle waiting outside the classroom with a bag of breakfast muffins from Zee's place.

"Oh, thanks," I said, taking the muffin she offered and biting into it.

"Don't tell Mum," said Estelle. "I had a couple of errands to run and I couldn't resist. How was your lesson?"

"Better than my attempt to get to it," I admitted.

Estelle tried not to laugh at my tale of the saga of the slide and the ball pit, but when I mentioned Sylvester's garbage chute remark, she lost it.

"Oh, sorry about that," she said between giggles. "Maybe the library's a bit distressed because of all the change. The murder, the crow... didn't Jet help you out?"

"I have no idea where he went," I said. "Hope he didn't get lost." That was all I needed—to lose my familiar before I even started.

"He'll be fine," she said. "He has wings. That's an advantage on the rest of us."

I bit into my muffin and sighed happily as the sweet taste filled my mouth. It was probably unhealthy, but I'd had a stressful week—and morning—so I figured I deserved it.

"So, what's on the agenda for today?" I asked, walking with her through the archives.

"You'll be shadowing Aunt Adelaide," she said. "Fair warning: she's in a mood today, since my dad invited himself over for dinner tonight."

"Oh, right, she said yesterday," I said. "Er, when you say she's in a mood, do you mean she's about to start throwing books at the late fee guy?"

"Oh, she doesn't reach Cass levels, but my sister got that temper from somewhere. Don't worry, she won't take it out on you."

It was with some trepidation that I walked to meet Aunt Adelaide at the front desk, but she gave me her usual smile. She wore more make-up than she had yesterday and her auburn hair looked shinier than usual. "How was it?"

"Not too bad," I said. "Aunt Candace seems unimpressed with the magical testing system."

"Oh, she gave you her speech." She rolled her eyes. "She's not wrong on some of it, but the academy can't go around handing out wands without checking basic knowledge first. You just have to pass the one theory exam before you get yours, so it won't be long before you can join proper classes."

I nodded. "And—biblio-witchery?"

"I'm having a book made up for you," she said. "Your Biblio-Witch Inventory contains the magic of the library itself, so it's likely to take a few more days. Estelle, can you check the returns?" she called. "Wouldn't want to send you to the Dimensional Studies section again, Rory."

I'd almost take that one over the ball pit.

For the rest of the morning, I returned books to shelves and occasionally helped Estelle track down an obscure title in one of the library's dark corners. When a satyr required a volume from the Magical Creatures Division, I made my way up to the third floor alone for the first time since my misadventures in the Dimensional Studies Section.

The Magical Creatures Division lay behind one of the closed doors at the back. Rustling, clicking and squeaking noises came from within, and a sign said, 'Staff Only Beyond This Point. Watch out for the Chimera.'

Hmm. Maybe I should have brought backup. I pushed the door open and almost collided with Cass coming the other way, a book tucked under her arm.

"Oh, sorry," I said.

"Don't you ever look before walking?" she snapped, stepping around me.

"What're you doing in here?"

"None of your business." She walked away, still holding the book tightly. *Really.* I remembered what Estelle had said about her keeping a new pet in here, but beyond the door lay a room filled with yet more shelves, and thankfully not a chimera in sight. Some of the books had fur or teeth, though, while others were locked in cages. At least four sealed doors at the back were marked with X symbols. I quickly found the book I needed and hurried out of there.

When Aunt Adelaide let me leave for lunch, I went out get some air. Maybe I'd walk to the bakery again… that was in danger of becoming a habit. The library wasn't stuffy, but I had a whole town to explore outside.

I crossed the square and walked down the road towards the coast. Even from behind the clock tower, the library's magnificent form loomed above the rest of the town. I walked along the seafront, enjoying the feel of the breeze in my hair—until I saw a male figure with a scythe strapped to his back reflected in the window of the shop on my left.

The Reaper was right behind me and I hadn't even

noticed. How did he walk that quietly? Must be a perk of being the angel of death. Xavier didn't *look* like the Grim Reaper. He wasn't even wearing a coat, just a plain black T-shirt and jeans that made his hair look even more golden than usual.

I turned to look at him. "You're on your way to collect another body?"

"Not at the moment, no," said Xavier. "Were you on your way to the beach?"

"Just walking. You're not here to claim my soul?"

He caught up, his steps swift and his eyes a startling aquamarine. "If I said yes, would it make you less afraid of me?"

"I'm not afraid." A blatant lie. But come on, he was carrying a scythe in broad daylight. More than a few people stepped aside as we walked past.

"Have you tried the ice cream?" He indicated a shop on my right. "It's the best in the region."

Ice cream. The Reaper was talking to me about ice cream. "No, it's freezing enough as it is. How do you not catch your death of cold without a coat? Is it some kind of Grim Reaper thing?"

"My mentor is the one who's known as the Grim Reaper. I'm more of a Mildly Annoyed Reaper."

"Mildly annoyed… why? Because of Duncan's missing soul?" Wait, why was I even bringing that up?

"That's part of it," he said. "My boss gave me a chewing-out over the situation even though he knows full well that the library isn't exactly… predictable."

"What, you think the library stole his soul?"

"Oh, no. I meant weird things happen there. I heard you and your cousin were investigating?"

Ah. So that's why he wanted to speak to me. He wanted his missing soul back.

"We hit a dead end," I admitted. "Estelle and I went to see

the last person who checked out the book—Alice, from the familiar shop—and she told us she loaned it to the curse-breaker last week to help him with a client. But he refused to tell us who it was."

"Oh, he would," said Xavier. "Not a fan of the library, he isn't."

"I worked that much out," I said. "So it's not common for a soul to go missing through a curse?"

"No, it's rare," he said. "I've been asking around myself, but I haven't found any leads. I sometimes provide evidence to Edwin if the souls I help move on remember how they died, but the problem this time is that the soul isn't there to begin with."

"I can see why that'd be an issue." The chill breeze from the coast stirred my hair and I shivered. On the beach, the sand looked clean, unlike most English beaches I'd been to, but the clouds gathering overhead promised rain later.

"Not really the weather to go paddling in the sea," he commented. "Another time, maybe."

"Does the Reaper go paddling in the sea?" I asked.

"Sure." He grinned. "I have to go. I'll see you around, Rory."

And he was gone scythe and all. He walked at such a fast pace, I'd have serious trouble keeping up with him. Also, I didn't remember telling him to call me Rory.

Books, I could read. People were trickier. Had he been chatting me up, or was he was just being friendly? Or trying to find out what I knew about the missing soul? I'd had a couple of boyfriends while I'd been at university, but I'd had no social life the last three years. Laney had tried to set me up with her brother, which had been a disaster, but other-wise, I'd been alone. And to be honest, I hadn't missed the stress of the dating game, with its million unspoken rules and constant misunderstandings. The odds of two people liking each other at the same time seemed so low, it had always baffled me how anyone found a partner at all, but most people I knew seemed to manage it.

Still, he'd been friendly. And not at all grim. Paddling in the sea indeed. The mental image of him standing in the water with his scythe made me grin. Definitely not the time to be daydreaming, Rory. Time to go back to the library.

I popped into the bakery on the way past. Once again, Zee stood behind the counter, which contained even more cards and bouquets of flowers than before. Either Duncan had been incredibly popular, or it was just that everyone knew and liked Zee.

"Hey," I said to her.

She gave me a strained smile. "Hey… Aurora?"

"Call me Rory," I said. "I'll take one of those sandwiches and a box of those cookies."

"Done. I wondered if I could ask a favour?" Zee said, packing cookies into a box. "There's a book I wanted to get from the library, but I haven't had time—without Duncan, I'm run off my feet until I find a new assistant. It's called *Cooking up a Storm*."

"Oh, sure," I said. "That's no problem."

She handed me the bag of goodies. "Thanks for coming over yesterday. I know you're new in town and didn't know Duncan, but he'd appreciate it."

"Ah, no worries." Guilt squirmed inside me. We'd made zero progress on finding out what'd cursed him, and while that wasn't my job, I couldn't help feeling I could have done more to help out.

When I got back to the library, I found Aunt Candace at the front desk, looking bored. "You're back. And you brought cookies."

"Yep." I offered her the bag and she took one. "Zee asked me to fetch a copy of *Cooking up a Storm*."

I pulled out the master list and scanned it, but I didn't see that particular title. "It's not here."

"Third floor," Aunt Candace said. "No—second. I think."

I put the bag of cookies down on the desk. "Never mind. I'll ask Aunt Adelaide."

"I wouldn't," she said. "She's cleaning. With magic." She shuddered. "The entire kitchen will be glowing by the time Elliot gets here."

"Oh. Where's Estelle?"

"Trying to rein her in. Unless you want a bath in a cleaning spell, Rory, I'd suggest you avoid that area for a bit."

"Noted." Okay, I could find the book by myself. The list told me magical cookbooks were on the ground floor, which I knew pretty well by this point. How hard could it be?

I walked through the stacks, scanning the shelves on either side. The magical cookbooks were on the right, so I headed that way. Checking the master list again, I counted rows. One, two—

The floor collapsed. A startled yell escaped as I flailed, my hands grasping for the nearest edge and finding none. The air rushed past, darkness closed in, and then my body landed on a soft surface. A mattress.

"How thoughtful." I lay on my back, my heart hammering. A single light illuminated the room, showing me a trapdoor above my head. It was far too high for me to reach.

I jumped off the mattress, looking around. The only other object in the room was a coffin. More worrying, it had no lid... and a person was inside it.

Ignoring the alarm bells wailing in my head, I trod towards the coffin. A man lay on his back, his eyes closed. I clapped my hands to my mouth. Was he *dead?* The man had dark hair and pale skin. His mouth was slightly open... and his teeth were pointed.

"Oh my god," I whispered. Estelle had told me vampires

didn't have heartbeats and slept like the literal dead. I didn't know if all the stories were true—the vampires who'd chased me had been wandering around during daylight hours, after all—but sleeping in coffins sounded like the sort of thing vampires did. If so...

Cold sweat gathered on my forehead. If he woke up, the first thing he'd see would be me. Then what would he do? I looked for another way out, but there were no doors or windows. Just the trapdoor.

I walked back to the mattress and stood on tip-toe, but my hands hardly brushed the ceiling If I called for help, I might wake the sleeping man in the coffin. By now, I was positive he must be alive. My aunts wouldn't keep a dead vampire in the basement, would they? Granted, I couldn't think of a good reason for them to keep a *living* vampire in here, either.

Even if he didn't wake up, I might be stuck here for hours waiting for someone to rescue me. *Think, Rory.* I didn't have a wand yet, but I was a biblio-witch—or I would be, anyway. That had to count for something, right?

I dug in my pocket and found the notebook and pen from my study lesson. In the shop, I'd put out the fire using Abe's record book and a cheap pen. It was worth a shot.

I pressed the tip of the pen to the page and focused on the words I wrote. *Fly. Make me fly.*

Nothing happened. I concentrated harder, searching for that wild urge that had possessed me when the vampires had cornered me—the *need* to write on the page.

Warmth flared within me, my skin tingled all over—and my body left the ground, yanked up through the trapdoor. *Whoa. Stop!*

My body kept floating, propelled down the row of shelves until I sailed around the corner and crashed into Cass.

"What are you doing?" we both asked, more or less at the same time.

"Nothing," she said.

"Why is there a vampire in the basement? What is going on?"

"Oh," she said, then swore. "This is why we don't invite newcomers here, so we don't have to explain Grandma's nonsense."

"What, it's her fault there's a vampire sleeping down there? He *is* still alive, right?"

She scowled. "Yes, he is. He came here before Grandma died, fell asleep, and never woke up. Vampires can hibernate for years."

I climbed to my feet, relieved that they stayed on the ground this time. "Who is he?"

"Grandma took that secret to her grave." She flicked her gaze to the trapdoor. "Just like all the others."

Whoa. She was serious. Not only was there an actual live vampire sleeping in the library's basement, nobody knew who he was. Two dead bodies in as many days—even if one of those bodies was *un*dead—was far more than I'd bargained for.

Cass pulled out her Biblio-Witch Inventory and stabbed at a word, causing the trapdoor to slam shut. "Do *not* tell anyone outside of our family. Got it?"

"Sure." Despite her warning tone, this was the most open Cass had ever been with me. Maybe, with each secret the library revealed to me, we'd be able to trust one another in the end.

Or maybe I was more likely to become buddies with the vampire in the basement.

———

I'd forgotten we were having a visitor, but when the library closed for the night, Aunt Adelaide called all of us to the front desk. She wore a new-looking cloak in vibrant shades of blue, her hair shone brighter than before, and she snapped her fingers, turning the library into night mode. Lights bloomed in the lanterns, mingling with the effect of the stained-glass windows.

A moment later, the doorbell rang. "Punctual as ever," she muttered. "One thing he got right."

Asking my aunts about the vampire would have to wait. Cass had implied they hadn't told the public about that one, though Estelle had also said that Aunt Adelaide's ex-husband had lived here in the library when they'd been together.

The doors opened, and Elliot entered the library. He wore a suit, which I hadn't expected, and wouldn't have looked out of place in an office in London. His face was severe, his hair well-combed, and his suit looked like it'd been ironed while he was still wearing it. He stood in stark contrast to my cloak-wearing aunts and cousins.

"Hey, Dad," said Estelle.

"Hello, honey." His gaze went to me. "Ah, this is the newcomer."

"Hi. I'm Aurora—most people call me Rory."

"Pleasure to meet you," he said, then turned to Aunt Adelaide. "Yes, I see the resemblance. She looks like Roger."

I shifted awkwardly, unsure what to say. He'd known my dad, too. I suspected it'd take me a while to adjust to the knowledge that he'd had an entire world he'd kept secret from me.

"I think she looks more like Adelaide," Aunt Candace said. "Maybe it's the nose."

Aunt Adelaide cleared her throat. "The table's set. Won't you come in?"

This is going to be awkward.

When we were seated in the dining room, Cass came in late, grunted at everyone and started eating without further conversation. I dug into my food, but I didn't have much of an appetite after the scare I'd had with the vampire.

Elliot turned to me. "So how are you finding the library?"

"It's..." Impossible to summarise in a single word. "Different."

"That's one way of putting it," he said. "When I met Adelaide, it used to find it amusing to turn the corridors around so I'd be walking in circles for hours."

"Yeah, it's tried some of that with me," I said. Over my dead body would I bring up the ball pit incident. "I guess I'll get used to it."

Cass made a disparaging noise, and silence fell for a few moments.

"Go on, ask about the murder," said Aunt Candace. "I'm collapsing under the weight of the unicorn in the room."

"Candace," said Aunt Adelaide. "That's not appropriate dinner conversation."

"I assumed it was, since you cancelled your date for it."

Aunt Adelaide scowled at her. "You're in an unusually chatty mood. Finished a book, did you?"

"Yes, I did," Aunt Candace said. "Don't ask me about it."

"You brought it up yourself, three times," said Cass, reaching for the salt. "Let's all ask Aunt Candace about her book. Better than Mum's love life."

Aunt Adelaide's face flushed, while Aunt Candace gave her a glare. At her side, I glimpsed her note-taking pen scribbling away out of sight.

Aunt Adelaide saw it, too, and gave her sister a blistering look. "If you write us into a book, I'll hex your pages blank."

Oh, boy. An argument was about to kick off and it wasn't even between her and her ex-husband.

Estelle stood. "I have to go and study. So does Rory."

I took her lead and got to my feet, too. We escaped into the living room, as the sound of glass breaking came from the room.

Estelle winced. "I'll have to intervene. You can get up to your room okay, right? Give me a shout if not."

I opened my mouth to respond, but she hurried back to the dining room as another crash came from behind the half-open door. Walking to the stairs, I found them gone. *Great.*

All right, I'd hide in the main library instead. I made for the Reading Corner, and a small pair of beady yellow eyes looked up at me from the shelf on my right.

"Caw," said Jet.

"There you are," I said to the crow. "What's wrong?"

He tapped the book next to him with his beak. I crouched to peer at the title and found none. The leather-bound book was Dad's journal. What was it doing all the way down here?

"Did Sylvester move this?" The owl might not be my biggest fan, but messing with my personal possessions seemed a bit much even for him.

The crow fluffed his feathers, looking agitated. I tucked the journal under my arm. I hadn't thought to see if my room had a lock, and I'd left in a hurry that morning, but I'd assumed the journal was in my rucksack where I'd left it. Who'd moved it? Only my family even knew it existed.

The crow flew to land on my shoulder. If nothing else, I was glad of the company. The library held far more secrets than I'd expected, and today had been as filled with surprises as the previous one. Yet despite the hair-raising start I'd had, I couldn't imagine myself anywhere but here.

9

T he next morning, the library thought it was funny to turn the corridor outside my room into a staircase. Every time I reached the top, another set of stairs waited for me. Just what I needed after a night of bad dreams of falling into the vampire's basement. Except in my dream, I'd fallen into a room containing the vampires from Dad's shop, and the coffin, which was empty, had my name on it.

So much for a relaxing start to the weekend.

Estelle rescued me on the fifth corridor.

"Rory! This way. Cut that out," she said sternly, addressing the library in general. She stood in front of a door which I recognised as my own room's.

"You mean I never left the corridor?" I sighed. "First my dad's journal goes missing and now this. Where *is* Jet?"

"Haven't a clue," said Estelle. "You sound like you need a whole pot of coffee in you. Also, what do you mean, your dad's journal went missing?"

"Someone took it," I said. "I found it on the shelf downstairs and I've never taken it out of my room."

"Maybe the library moved it," she said. "Trying to shelve it. It can pick up on the presence of other books in here. We usually have to give warning before bringing in books from outside. You brought some, didn't you?"

"Yes..." I stopped. "Oh, is that why it keeps pranking me whenever I try to leave my room?"

"Possibly," she said. "Maybe it needs time to learn to trust you."

We headed downstairs to the kitchen.

"It's a bit difficult for me to return that trust when I keep falling into basements containing sleeping vampires," I said.

"Vampires?" She pushed open the kitchen door and walked in. "Oh, you found Albert."

"That's his name? Cass didn't say." I found two mugs filled with coffee that someone had left out on the side, along with two plates of toast. "What's this, a peace offering after last night?"

"I'd guess so." She picked up a mug and plate. "I've never seen Mum and Aunt Candace go at it like that for a while. Cass didn't help. Did you say you talked to her?"

"I ran into her on the way out of the basement." I picked up the other mug, taking a sniff. Extra strong coffee. Aunt Adelaide must have been taking notes on me. "She said Grandma knew he was there."

"Oh, yeah." Estelle led the way into the living room and sat down. "We call him Albert, but we don't know his actual name. Mum said she never met him before."

"She never..." I trailed off. "You have a vampire in your basement and you don't know who he is or how he got there?"

"Well, no," she admitted, taking a bite of toast. "I know, it's odd. Beyond odd, but that pretty much sums up Grandma. She *did* create the library, after all."

"No kidding." I bit into my own piece of toast. "I'm still

kind of lost on how you managed to go for years without knowing there was a vampire sleeping underneath your feet."

"Oh, we found him when I was a toddler," she said. "I fell through the trapdoor by accident."

I choked on my toast. "What, you mean he was there before you were born?"

"Grandma would never admit it, but it must have been."

"And it's normal for vampires to take decades-long naps?" I swallowed my mouthful. "Wish the ones hunting for Dad's journal would do the same." Last night's dream was a little too recent to make jokes about vampires.

"They won't find you here," she said. "This is the safest place you could possibly be. From vampires, anyway."

"Except the one in the basement."

"Relax. If he was going to wake up, he would have done so when Cass was arguing with Samson the other day."

I sipped my coffee. "Is Samson permanently banned?"

"No, we rarely issue full bans. The library's used for too many functions and other events. I know for a fact Samson wanted to perform at the next poetry night... I think Duncan would have wanted it to go ahead. How did you end up finding the basement, anyway?"

"I was looking for a book for Zee," I explained. "*Cooking up a Storm*. I never did find it."

"Oh, I'll handle that," she said. "How did you get out of the vampire's room?"

"I used magic." I put down my mug. "I was going to tell you last night, but everyone was a bit distracted."

"That's one way of putting it," she said. "You used bibliowitchery again?"

I nodded. "It works with any pen and paper?"

"It works better with our specially designed ones, but in a pinch, your magic will always come through for you," she said.

When we'd finished breakfast, I went with her to get the book for Zee. This time, the floor didn't give way, and we retrieved the book without any encounters with vampires, sleeping or otherwise. But handing it over to Zee would have to wait. The instant the library doors opened, an influx of academy students swarmed in, ready to argue over the limited copies of textbooks to write their essays at the last minute. Estelle had to run around breaking up fights all morning, while I fetched copies of every textbook on the university's reading list.

I stood on a ladder, reaching for a book on one of the higher shelves, when someone cleared his throat behind me.

"Can you pass me that?" Dominic asked, pointing at the fifth shelf.

"Sure." I wasn't sure I'd ever get used to the way vampires moved. Then again, the Reaper moved just as swiftly and silently. I pulled down the book he'd asked for—*Curses and Charms, Volume Five.*

"Are you sure you should be checking out books on curses so recently after Duncan's murder?" I asked.

"Why, has Edwin come back?" he asked. "Last I heard, he was questioning Duncan's close family."

"Is one of them likely to have cursed him?" I'd forgotten to ask Aunt Candace if she'd made any more progress on the book after yesterday's disastrous meal with Elliot.

"I haven't the faintest clue." He gave the book's cover a scan. "Hmm. I suppose it is in bad taste. I'll ask Mr Bennet instead. He probably knows about the fang-shrinking curse."

"That's what you wanted it for? Shrinking your own fangs? Or someone else's?"

"They do get in the way sometimes." He handed me the book back, and in a flash, he was gone. *Vampires.*

I found the textbook I'd been searching for, hopped off the ladder, and made my way through the crowded Reading

Corner. Dominic hadn't picked the best timing to ask for a book on curses, though admittedly, people in the magical world probably looked them up all the time.

I handed the textbook to the student who'd asked for it, spotting Samson sitting apart from the others. Judging by the small mountain of books beside him, he had no intention of returning any of them.

Speaking of returns… I had no business making assumptions, but it wouldn't hurt to see if Dominic's story held up.

I walked to the front desk and picked up the record book. He hadn't returned anything today… hang on a minute. He'd mentioned Mr Bennet. Might Dominic be the curse-breaker's client, the one Mr Bennet had refused to tell me about? That didn't immediately make either of them guilty, but if Mr Bennet had borrowed the book in order to help his client, perhaps Dominic had handled it before Duncan's death. Had he told the police?

I walked to the front doors and opened them, then halted on the doorstep. I'd never catch up to the vampire on foot. Never mind. He'd be back in the library before long.

A gust of wind crashed into me and a man appeared from thin air just in front of the doorstep.

A vampire—*not* Dominic. It was the man from the shop, who'd called himself Mortimer Vale. One of the vampires who'd been after Dad's journal.

He disappeared again, and I felt a hand close over my mouth. He'd moved behind me in a heartbeat, stopping me from getting back into the library. I grabbed for the door handle, but he caught my hand before it could make contact. A scream rose in my throat, cut off by his other hand.

"Quiet, little girl."

"I'm not—a child," I said, my voice muffled. Great comeback there, Rory. "Let me go!"

"You're a child to us," he purred in my ear. "And you won't

be going back into that library until you listen to what I have to say."

"I won't help you." I bit his hand and gave another muffled yelp of pain. Ow. His skin was like concrete.

He wrenched my arm behind my back, and I whimpered.

"What you're going to do," he said, "is fetch that journal. You know what journal I mean. You're going to bring it to me, and you're not going to tell anyone. That clear?"

"You're breaking my arm!" I gasped, drawing in a breath for another scream.

"Humans are so breakable," he grumbled, pushing me towards the door. "Go."

The instant he let go of my arm, I grabbed my pen and notebook from my pocket, gripping the pen between my fingertips. A rush of energy shot through my body as the pen touched the page—but I didn't know nearly enough about magic to know what spell could outdo a vampire.

"None of that." He bared his fangs. "They've taught you some tricks, have they? It won't help you. I hope you'll reconsider your choice. Otherwise, your library will be the next to burn."

In a blink, he was gone.

I stood rigidly, the pen and notebook still clutched in my hands. He was bluffing. The library was magical. He couldn't set it on fire, right? But—he shouldn't have been able to find me here. I was supposed to be safe.

I pushed open the doors to the library and nearly collided with Estelle.

"I wondered where you'd gone." She held a smoking wand in her hand, and her hair stood on end. "Two students got into a fight over the last remaining copy of the *Advanced Companion to Magical Theory*... Rory, what's wrong?"

"I ran into one of those vampires." I pushed my notebook and pen back into my pocket, my hands shaking. "He—

threatened to set the place on fire if I didn't hand over my dad's journal."

Her eyes widened. "What? Where?"

I pointed over my shoulder with a trembling hand. "He appeared from nowhere and threatened me. And now he'll be after all of us."

I was babbling, but I couldn't help it. My mind spun in circles. The vampire must have contact with someone in town. It was isolated, miles from my former home... but the paranormal world was smaller than the normal one. Had someone told him I was living here now? Another of the local vampires, maybe? His two companions hadn't been with him.

Why did they want the journal so badly?

Estelle fetched Aunt Adelaide and dragged her into the kitchen, where she fussed around making me a mug of calming herbal tea while I explained my narrow escape.

"There were three of them." I sipped the tea, warmth chasing away the chill. I'd barely been outside a minute, but it felt like the cold sea breeze had gone right into my bones. "They want Dad's journal, and they followed me all the way here. How?"

Aunt Adelaide pursed her lips. "Maybe... they must have followed our trace when we used magic to scare them off."

"They didn't need to," Estelle said. "Come on, there aren't many biblio-witches out there. They'll have contacts in other paranormal communities. We never found out where they came from."

"His name's Mortimer Vale," I said. "He told me last time. I should have said."

"The name doesn't ring a bell," Aunt Adelaide said. "Besides, he won't get into the library. It's warded against hostile intent."

"Then how did that cursed book get in?" I took another long sip of tea.

"Books are trickier," she responded. "But people like him are *not* welcome here."

"If not, we could always dig a moat," I said. "I mean, uh, the water rule applies here, too, right? I wouldn't have thought they'd want to live in a town on the coast."

"Oh, they're definitely not local," Aunt Adelaide said firmly. "And we'll run them out of town when we find where they're staying."

"They might not be staying here, though," I said. "Given how quickly he moves, he might be miles away by now."

"He told you to bring him the journal, didn't he?" Estelle said. "That suggests he's staying in town. There are only so many places he could be hiding. I'll call the local hotels, for a start."

"I don't understand how those vampires even know about the journal," I admitted, drinking more tea. I felt calmer, but no less confused.

"Where is it now?" asked Aunt Adelaide.

"In my room." *I hope.* Maybe I should have carried it with me after it'd disappeared yesterday, but if I had, the vampire might have snatched it off me there and then.

"Let me have a look at it later," said Aunt Adelaide. "In the meantime, I'll report him to the police."

"He threatened to set the place on fire if I told anyone," I said, a fresh shiver of fear fighting against the effect of the calming tea.

"The hell he will." Estelle looked disgusted. "This place is protected against every kind of magical disaster possible. That vampire has no idea what he's messing with."

"Trust me, we're prepared for every eventuality." Aunt Adelaide rose to her feet. "I'll give Edwin a call. Estelle, call the local hotel owners. We have to show we aren't afraid."

But I am *afraid.* My own magical newbie nature aside, vampires were terrifying. "I'd never have got away if he hadn't wanted me to fetch the journal."

Estelle gave me a sympathetic nod. "Believe me, I know how scary they can be. I'll call Frederick. He runs the local B&B, he'll know if there's anyone around who shouldn't be. Besides, any gossip will reach the library eventually."

I hope you're right. None of the chatting students or other patrons showed any signs of fear. Then again, vampires were a normal sight to them. They wouldn't know the terror of being confronted by one of them as a helpless human without magic.

Estelle made the call, while I drank the rest of the calming tea. After a few minutes of questions, she hung up.

"Nobody new has checked into the B&B in the last two days," she said. "Frederick said he hasn't seen any unfamiliar faces around."

"That's probably because the vampire moves so fast, nobody can see his face," I said. "How can even a witch outdo a vampire?"

"You'd be surprised," Estelle said. "Trust me, you'll feel a lot more prepared when you've learned more magic. Anyway, I think we should contact the leader of the local vampires and let him know there's a rogue on the loose in town. Then the other vampires will chase him off."

"Oh," I said, thinking of Dominic. "Well, Dominic was here, but he took off, too. Also…" I hesitated.

"Also what?" she asked.

"Uh, he was looking at books on curses," I said. "I think he's the client the curse-breaker was covering for. He mentioned meeting with him today."

"Ah, really?" She frowned. "He's lived here for years. Those other vampires, though, they're not local. And we'll run them out of town, count on it."

Until then, no more wandering around alone. Not until those vampires were long gone.

———

I'd intended to go and have another look at the journal as soon as possible, but errands kept me busy for the rest of the afternoon. I was glad to have something to take my mind off the vampire's threat, but his fanged face remained in the back of my mind.

As the library closed its doors for the night, Aunt Adelaide snapped her fingers and called all of us into the lobby. All of us except Cass, that is, who'd pulled another of her disappearing acts.

"Rory has been threatened," she announced.

"She has?" Aunt Candace asked. "By who?"

"The same vampires as before," I said. "They followed me here. One of them did, anyway."

A muscle ticked in Aunt Candace's jaw. "That won't do at all. Have you told the local vampires?"

"I sent word to them." Aunt Adelaide wrinkled her nose. "I've asked around and nobody can confirm if there's a strange vampire staying in the town or not, but he wants Roger's journal."

"Roger's journal?" Aunt Candace asked. "Oh, right, that one. I can't say I know if he made enemies with vampires, but maybe there's a clue inside the journal somewhere. It must be valuable." Interest dripped from her words. At least someone would get a good story out of my dilemma.

"It's written in code," I reminded her. "I can fetch it, but I've never been able to read it and neither has anyone else."

"We'll have a look at it, then," Aunt Adelaide said. "And just where is Cass hiding?"

"Haven't a clue," said Estelle. "I'll find her."

"And I'll fetch the journal." I walked to the stairs, peering up to make sure there weren't any obstacles in the way. There came a faint cawing from above, then Jet flew to land on my shoulder. I hadn't seen my familiar all day, so I assumed he didn't know about the vampire threatening me.

"Hey," I said to him. "I'm going to my room to fetch the journal. Is it there?"

The crow made an odd chirping noise, tugging on my sleeve. I got the message and climbed the stairs.

The door to my room lay partly open. I pushed it inwards, my heart sinking a little. Everything appeared to be in place—with one exception.

The journal was gone.

10

I looked around my bedroom, scanning every corner. Then I pulled titles off the bookshelves, checking each one on the off-chance that I'd put the journal there and forgotten.

The journal wasn't in my room. Either someone had taken it, or the library had tried to play yet another trick on me. Not great timing, considering the threat the vampire had made. Aunt Adelaide had called the library semi-sentient, so you'd think it'd be aware by now that someone wished us harm, but I'd found the journal downstairs before. Maybe the library had tried to shelve it again.

I turned to Jet, who sat on the bedpost watching me. "Did you hear what my aunts said about the vampire?" I asked him. "He threatened the library. And me. I think we should stick together from now on."

I held out a hand, and the crow chirped and landed on it. There'd be time to train my familiar later, but right now, I needed to find that missing journal.

Of course, there was one other possibility—someone had

taken it to give to the vampire, so he'd leave us alone. Cass's face came to mind. Even she wouldn't be *that* mean, right? But I *had* seen her carrying a small, square book under her arm earlier. Had she been sneaking peeks at the journal, or was I letting our mutual dislike cloud my judgement?

I left my room, with Jet still sitting on my shoulder.

"Hey," I said to the library in general. "If you know where the journal is, it would be great if you could show me where to find it. I don't know if you can understand me, but someone wants to get his hands on that book, and if I don't give it to him, he threatened to burn you down."

The library did not respond. But it didn't take away the stairs on my way back down, either. I hurried back to join my family in the lobby.

They weren't alone. Edwin the elf stood beside a rather windswept Cass.

"Your daughter was trespassing on private property," he said to Aunt Adelaide.

Cass scowled. "It wasn't trespassing. Nobody lives on the pier."

"The pier is out of bounds when the tides are in," the elf said sternly. "You could have been swept out to sea."

She gave a disparaging snort. "I wouldn't be much of a witch if I was scared of a little water."

The chief of police shook his head at Aunt Adelaide. "She refuses to tell me *why* she was on the pier on a freezing winter day when the tide was out."

"Maybe I wanted to go for a swim?" Cass said.

Aunt Adelaide sighed. "Cass, apologise to Edwin. Really, how old are you?"

"Sorry, Edwin," Cass said, not sounding sorry. "Searching me wasn't necessary."

"For all I knew, you were out to vandalise the place,"

Edwin said. "Adelaide, please discipline your daughter. No charges will be pressed today."

"I'm honoured," Cass said, and Aunt Adelaide gave her a warning look.

Hmm. Cass hadn't even been inside the library today. The book had definitely been in my room this morning, and if she'd been on the pier, she couldn't have been meeting with the vampire. Not when they hated water so much.

The image of Mortimer Vale on the bridge came to mind and I fought a shudder. He hadn't seemed *afraid* of the water, more annoyed that I'd eluded him. And he was here in town somewhere.

I hurried over to the elf policeman before he left. "Hey, Edwin, did my aunt call you about the vampire in town who shouldn't be?"

"Yes, I heard your aunt's complaints," he said. "Both times. Don't worry. The vampires will gain nothing from threatening the most magically protected place in town."

"But—they were trying to steal my dad's old journal," I said. "And I just found out it's missing."

"Did you want to file a complaint?" he asked. "Miss Hawthorn, you live in a library. Perhaps you misplaced the book among the many other titles on your shelves."

He was right: I should at least check the whole library before I threw accusations around. Besides, if the vampire got the journal, he wouldn't come after me again. He'd have no reason to if he already had what he wanted.

———

The following day was Sunday, so I slept in late and woke feeling refreshed despite my failure to find the journal yesterday evening. Estelle and I had searched the entire ground floor, but it was impossible to check every title. I got out of bed and checked my room again in case it'd reappeared overnight. No such luck.

Cass had refused to help me search, to no surprise, but hadn't exhibited any signs of guilt either. It was entirely possible Aunt Candace had swiped the journal for book research purposes or something, but she knew how serious the vampire's threat was. That left Sylvester, who'd come when I'd called his name, told me he wasn't in charge of lost property, and swooped off again.

The library wasn't open to the public on Sunday, giving me free rein to search as much as I liked. I wouldn't have minded grabbing a muffin from Zee's place, but I'd avoid going outside alone until the vampire was definitely gone.

I went into the kitchen and found Estelle buttering toast.

"Hey," she said. "I made coffee."

"You're a lifesaver." I picked up the mug she indicated on the sideboard. "The journal didn't show up in my room overnight."

"It's in here somewhere." She stuck more bread in the toaster. "Mum ordered me to go to every hotel in town in case the vampire's using a disguise, so that's my task of the day."

"Will you be okay?" I asked. "I know it's me he's after, but he's creepy and dangerous."

"I'm prepared." She tapped a page in her Biblio-Witch Inventory and the toast jumped onto a plate, which floated to me. "I'll be wearing a disguise of my own, for a start. Vampires might have a lot of talents, but they can't use magic the way we can."

I walked with her to the living room. "I guess not, but they can still threaten to burn libraries down."

"He won't get past the front door," she said. "Also, Aunt Candace is in the reference section looking up this Mortimer

Vale character. Since he's a vampire, he's probably centuries old and they always seem to find their way into the history books at one time or other."

"Right, that's why Dominic was fact-checking.' I never did get to visit the curse-breaker again, but there was no chance I'd be going there alone after yesterday. "Anyway, I guess I'll keep looking for the journal. I wish I knew what my dad actually wrote in there. That might tell us where the library decided to shelve it." If a magical library could read a code nobody else could, that is.

"Ask Sylvester to help out," she said. "Or Jet."

"Sure." I munched my toast. A free day… trapped indoors. Not that I was in the mood to tempt fate by wandering around outside with a murderous vampire on the loose. I just wished I could do something useful.

When I'd finished eating, I walked out to the lobby to find Xavier standing in front of the desk, his scythe thankfully tucked away behind his back.

"Oh, hi," I said. "You're not here to find another body, are you?"

"No," he said. "My boss is putting pressure on me, so I thought I'd come and have another look around. Your aunt invited me in. I won't make any trouble." He gave another of his dazzling smiles. Angel of death, indeed.

"I'm not sure my aunt's made any progress with the book," I admitted. "She's busy looking up the vampire today. Did Aunt Adelaide tell you?"

"Tell me what?"

"There's a vampire in town who shouldn't be. He's chasing me, because he wants this old journal my dad wrote before he died."

Xavier's eyes widened. "No, I didn't know that."

"I thought Aunt Adelaide was telling everyone she ran

into," I said. "My cousin is trying to track down where the vampire is staying."

"Did you say he was after your dad's old journal? Why?"

"Haven't a clue, but it's gone missing somewhere in the library," I said. "Estelle and I already checked most of the ground floor, but there's a million places it might be hidden."

"Want me to help look for it?" he said. "I'm heading over to the Reading Corner anyway."

"Sure."

In the Reading Corner, Tad was still in his usual hammock, asleep. Other than that, nobody was around, not even Samson. Xavier and I talked as we made our way through the fiction section. It turned out he was a fan of my aunt's books and knew all about her secret pen names. I admitted I hadn't read one yet, and he gave me a whole list of recommendations. Despite our lack of progress on the journal, my mood improved. I'd put it down to the coffee, but I couldn't remember the last time I'd had a real chance to get to know someone new. I'd met up with Laney a lot, but all I'd ended up doing was talking about Abe and the shop. Now the weight of responsibility had lifted, I felt... lighter.

Or maybe it was because the floor was moving.

Xavier gave me a grin. "I like this bit."

"I'm getting the impression you've been to this part of the library before." The floor continued to slide, conveyor-belt style, and I was glad my cloak stopped at ankle-length, or else I'd have tripped over the end. We glided across the floor, bookshelves flitting past on either side.

"I have." He spread his arms like wings and I burst out laughing at how ridiculous he looked.

"You can't actually fly, can you?"

"No, but I can glide." He took my arm and we slid past another row of shelves. "Want to jump off here? On three."

At the count of three, we jumped off the sliding floor, landing on an island between shelves.

"I swear I could live here a year and find a new corner every day," I said, catching my breath.

"Have they told you about the invisible section yet?"

I gave him a suspicious look. "Are you having me on?"

"Nope. A botched spell a few years ago turned a whole corridor invisible. Nobody's been able to find it since."

I stared at him, then cracked up laughing. "Honestly, you could be telling fibs and it still makes sense for this place."

He laughed, too. "I guess it does sound a bit outlandish to someone from outside this world."

"Considering you're a Reaper, I suppose nothing surprises you."

"Rarely, but it happens." His eyes were alight with mischief. "Besides, that was fun."

"More fun than most of the pranks the library's played on me this week," I admitted. "Yesterday, it got me stuck on an endless staircase."

I wondered if he knew about the sleeping vampire. I didn't want to wreck the mood by bringing up the threat to my life again, so we resumed our hunt for the journal until Sylvester ambushed us on the second floor.

"Your aunt has requested your presence downstairs," he said, eyeing Xavier. "Reaper, is it? Found your missing soul?"

"Not yet," said Xavier.

Sylvester tutted. "Losing a journal is one thing, but losing a soul is incredibly careless."

"You were here when it happened," I pointed out. "Also, I bet you could find my journal any time you wanted to."

"I have already expressed my thoughts on the subject," he said.

"Fine, I'll ask Jet," I said. "Maybe he'll find it before you do."

"He would never," the owl said indignantly, and departed in a swoop of wings.

"Oh, that's how I can persuade him to do things," I observed. "Offer him a little competition."

"Who's Jet?"

"My familiar. We'd better go see what my aunt wants."

My two aunts and Estelle waited by the front desk. This time, even Cass was there, arms folded across her chest, wearing a disdainful expression.

"There's been a new development," said Aunt Adelaide. "Candace has made progress on the book."

"I said, the opposite of progress," said Aunt Candace. "I got the book open. It's not cursed at all."

I stared at her. "Are you sure?"

Aunt Candace pulled the small book out of her pocket and held it up, turning it around so we could all see it. The little book of curses sat in her hand, deceptively harmless. She didn't drop dead or start screaming. After all that... the book wasn't cursed after all?

"Was it cursed just to harm Duncan and nobody else?" Estelle's brow crinkled.

"There'd still be traces left behind," said Aunt Candace. "Trust me, I'd know."

"Are you sure you didn't remove the curse yourself by accident?" Cass enquired.

"I couldn't remove the curse without removing the binding. There wasn't anything underneath it."

"Why would someone bind it shut, then?" Xavier asked.

"Exactly." Aunt Candace opened the book, and a slip of paper fell out. She quickly snapped the book closed to catch it before it hit the ground. "Maybe that's the reason."

"What is that?" I asked. We all moved to the front desk as Aunt Candace laid the book down, opening it to reveal the loose slip of paper.

"It's one of Duncan's poems, by the look of things," said Estelle. "Yes, I recognise it from the last poetry night. Three people feigned sickness to get out."

"I'm not surprised." Cass pointed at the opening line, which read, 'Let the nefarious rites begin.'

Aunt Candace tutted, snapping the book closed. "That's taken care of, then. The book isn't cursed. Something else killed the boy."

"But…" I said. "If the book didn't curse him, then what did?"

"Precisely," said Aunt Candace. If anything, she sounded excited at all the possibilities.

"Would the curse-breaker know?" I asked uncertainly.

Aunt Adelaide wrinkled her nose. "I doubt Mr Bennet will have anything useful to say, not if there wasn't a curse at all."

Xavier stepped in. "If it's okay with you, I can take Rory with me to visit the curse-breaker. I'll make sure nothing happens to her."

Cass snorted, and Estelle nudged her in the ribs.

Aunt Adelaide nodded. "Yes, if you'd like to get some fresh air. Best not to leave the library unaccompanied until the situation has been taken care of."

And that's how I found myself walking outside with the Reaper. As little as I wanted to wander around town when someone wanted me dead, even a vampire wouldn't mess with Xavier, with his scythe in plain view. We attracted a fair few stares as we walked. Most of them looked at Xavier, then me, with undisguised surprise.

"What're they gawking at us for?" I asked him in an undertone.

He shrugged. "You're new in town and you're hanging out with the Reaper."

"Am I supposed to run screaming? After the vampires, you're like a cuddly baby kitten."

He coughed a laugh. "I believe that's the first time anyone has ever described me using those words."

"It works," I said. "If you ignore the scythe, anyway."

"Most people can't ignore it. Hence the stares."

"Ah. Can't you like… leave it behind? You're not on soul-catching duty all the time, are you?"

He paused for a moment before answering. "The scythe is part of the deal even when I'm not on duty. I never know when I'm going to run into a soul in need of saving."

"Is that what your job is, then? Rescuing souls… to take them to the afterlife?"

"Essentially," he said. "I rarely need to *use* the scythe. I can hide it, but I thought it'd make any vampire think twice before attacking you."

Oh. As flattering as it might be to think he wanted to keep me safe, realistically, there was no reason for him to take the risk of running into murderous vampires other than to get one step closer to finding Duncan's missing soul.

We reached the road along the seafront. "The curse-breaker wasn't particularly nice to me last time. He doesn't like biblio-witches."

"Has he been questioned by the police?" he asked.

"Not that I know of. He claimed 'customer confidentiality' stopped him from telling me who hired him to help with a curse. I think it was that vampire, Dominic. But if the book wasn't cursed after all, it's irrelevant."

"It's worth asking him again." Xavier pushed open the door to the shop.

Like last time, the curse-breaker waited behind the desk, tall and thin and scowling.

"We close early on Sundays," Mr Bennet said.

"Not for an hour, last I checked," Xavier responded, his voice cheerful. "Terrible weather, isn't it?"

The curse-breaker visibly paled. "Reaper. To what do I owe the pleasure?"

"I'm here with her." He indicated me, his hand brushing my arm. Warmth heated my cheeks. *Well, now I know how to get the curse-breaker to take me seriously: bring the Reaper.*

"We have an update on the cursed book," I told Mr Bennet.

"I don't recall asking for one."

Okay... "I just thought you might be interested to know that the book *wasn't* cursed. My aunt broke open the sealing spell and there wasn't anything underneath."

He didn't even blink. "I thought so."

"What, you knew?" I frowned. "Since when?"

"It was the logical conclusion. One person was affected and no others. A book in a library might have been picked up by anyone."

"Then why seal it shut?" Had someone been trying to throw us off the trace, or was there something else hidden in the pages? I'd have to ask my aunt to know for sure. "You saw Dominic the vampire this week, right?"

"Customer confidentiality," he said, his tone downright bored.

"It seems to me that the police would be interested to know," said Xavier. "It's pertinent to their investigation, after all. Whether the book was involved or not, it was definitely a curse that killed Duncan."

Mr Bennet's face reddened. "What do you want to know?"

"You helped Dominic," I said. "He's the one you needed the book for, right? Why bring it here rather than checking it out of the library?"

"Because Alice already had it," the curse-breaker said. "Your library is very particular about the rules. When I heard

Alice had a book on advanced curses, I borrowed it to help Dominic look up a fang-shrinking curse. The book turned out to be unnecessary, so I returned it to Alice."

"And then she put it back in the library," I mused. "Did Duncan visit you before he died?"

"No," he said. "We've never spoken."

Hmm. "But he was looking up curses for a reason, right?"

His eyes narrowed. "We're a paranormal town. Maybe things are different wherever you came from, Miss Hawthorn, but most people deal with curses in their day-to-day lives without feeling the need to consult a curse-breaker, especially witches and wizards. I would expect your family to have told you so themselves rather than sending you to bother me with inane questions."

"That's enough," said Xavier sharply. "You have no reason to be rude to Rory."

"Never mind," I said. "He's right, I didn't know. But I know where *not* to come if I need help with curses."

I turned around and left the shop, marching down the road. Despite my furious pace, Xavier easily kept in step with me.

"Less than a week here and I'm already burning bridges." I muttered a curse—not of the magical variety. "He hated my grandmother. They argued over the library, according to Estelle."

"That's no excuse for the way he spoke to you," he said, with a disgruntled glance over his shoulder. "If you ask me, he was irritated because you reminded him that most witches and wizards don't actually need the help of a curse-breaker. A ten-year-old could remove a basic curse, so he's stuck working for people like that vampire."

"Ah, that explains it," I said. "I swear I wasn't trying to insult him. I'm just slow to learn the new rules here."

"You're doing fine," he said. "Considering you knew nothing at all about magic until a few days ago."

"There is that." If the book wasn't cursed, that opened up the case again... in theory. I'd read enough from the beginner's textbook to know some curses took a while to act. Which meant if someone had cast the curse on Duncan a week ago and timed it to go off at that particular moment, we might never know who did it.

My shoulders slumped.

"Something wrong?" Xavier asked.

I shook my head. "Curses can be set on a timer to go off weeks after they were cast. If it wasn't the book, it might have been anything that cursed him."

"That doesn't explain where Duncan's soul went," said Xavier. "If the curse was on an object, he'd have been touching it when he died, and if a person cast it, they'd need to be there in person."

"So the caster *was* there in the library?" That brought us to same list of suspects again. "What did they curse, then? He wasn't holding anything else. Unless they cursed his shoe or something."

Xavier shook his head. "No, only a powerful magical object can hold a person's soul. I assumed the boundary spells on the book held it captive, but I was wrong."

Ah. Being the person who dealt with souls, he was definitely the expert out of the two of us.

"Maybe a different book was cursed," I said. "And the murderer put that one in his hands to throw us off the trace."

"Huh. It's possible," he said. "I have to get pretty close to be able to pick up on the presence of a soul, and with so many books in the library, it'd be hard to pinpoint. At this rate, I'll have to bring my boss in."

"At least that might put off the vampires," I said.

His mouth tightened. "That vampire must know the

library is protected by the most powerful spells in the whole town, to say nothing of your aunts' power."

"Maybe, but vampires are faster and stronger than any person, by far, and they nearly got into the library once already."

"You got away twice, didn't you?" he asked. "I assume you did, since you're still in one piece."

"I did, but they let me go because they wanted my dad's journal," I said. "Which I managed to lose anyway. Not sure that counts as a victory."

"But you did use magic, right?" he said. "You put yourself down too much."

"Maybe I do," I admitted. Laney had said the same, but spending my days being berated by Abe for every reason under the sun had made me used to criticism and not so much to praise.

But he was right: I *had* used magic to get away from the vampire, and I wasn't even properly trained yet. "Now all I have to do is find a missing book in a library. There's a joke in there somewhere about needles and haystacks."

"I was refraining from making that one." He grinned. "Come on, I'll walk you back. My boss will be wondering where I am."

We made our way back from the seafront to the towering shape of the library. Already, I was starting to think of it as home. Now if only it would cooperate with me and help me find Dad's journal.

I waved goodbye to Xavier and entered the library, which was quieter than usual. A few of the regulars were around even though it was Sunday, but if not for the faint background noise of rustling pages, the place seemed deserted.

I walked in the direction of Aunt Candace's testing room where she'd been trying to break the curse on the book. If the book wasn't cursed, I was at a loss as to what might have caused Duncan's death. Much less where his soul had ended up.

The classroom door was slightly open. Frowning, I pushed it inwards, and there was a clunk as it connected with something hard.

The book of curses lay on the floor. So did a man's body, his hand inches away from the book, a lopsided green hat beside his head.

Tad, the local eccentric. He was dead.

I screamed. The sound didn't echo and nobody came running. There must be an alarm, right? Wait—the emergency button. I scrambled in my pocket for the piece of paper Estelle had given me on my first day and tapped the word *help.*

A wailing noise sprang from the paper, echoing up to the heights of the ceiling until the entire library reverberated with the noise. Then, Aunt Adelaide materialised on the spot.

"Rory, what—?" She broke off at the sight of Tad's body. "Oh, goddess."

"I found him like this," I said. "I just got back a minute ago."

We both looked at his sprawling, inert body, and the book lying half open beside him. What had he been doing, trying to sneak a look at the book of curses? Aunt Candace had touched it. It couldn't be cursed. But then—what had killed him?

"Who would kill him?" she said softly. "He was harmless."

"I know." I wrenched my gaze away from Tad's staring eyes and bright green hat. "Where's Aunt Candace? She must have left the room unlocked, and I guess he tried to take the book."

And someone had killed him for it.

"CANDACE!" Aunt Adelaide bellowed. "Sorry, she probably put her alarm on mute. She always does that when she's working. It's rare that we have an actual emergency."

"Cass and Estelle are out, then?" I asked. "So—is the killer still here? Would the library know if anyone left?"

"I knew I should have asked Sylvester to watch the doors," she said. "But he went to keep an eye on Estelle in case she ran into those vampires."

My stomach turned over. The place still looked deserted, though the sound of the alarm ought to have alerted everyone within hearing distance.

Was the killer still in the library? The book must be involved—there was no way it was a coincidence that it'd wound up next to two dead bodies—but if it wasn't cursed, then what had killed him?

Aunt Candace materialised next to us, an aggravated look on her face. "This had better be good."

Aunt Adelaide cleared her throat and indicated the body. "He was found here."

"I found him," I added.

Aunt Candace swore. "I thought I locked that door. What're we going to do with him?"

At that moment, the front door opened and Xavier strode in. "Hey, Rory," he said.

Ah. What was I supposed to say? 'Nice to see you' wouldn't cut in, since someone was dead. "Hi."

He spotted Tad's body and walked over, holding his scythe in both hands. There was a long pause, then he said, "I thought I felt his soul, but it's gone."

My heart sank. *Just like Duncan.*

"I found him here." I indicated the half-open door and the

book on the floor. "I think he picked up the book, but we already know it's not cursed."

Xavier paced around the body, frowning. "I think it's the same as the other time. Was he holding anything else?"

"No, I found him like that."

Xavier paused with his scythe poised over Tad's body, looking into space as though seeing something I couldn't. Then he shook his head. "No. His soul is definitely gone."

Aunt Adelaide cleared her throat. "If I had to guess, he came here to get the book and was ambushed from behind."

"No witnesses," I said. "When was the last time anyone came near this room, or through the Reading Corner? He's normally over there."

"I checked on the book first thing this morning," Aunt Candace said. "At least three hours ago. I've been working on my manuscript since then."

"I assumed Candace left the door locked so I haven't been here," Aunt Adelaide said. "Estelle's been out all day, and Cass has, too. I'll call the police. Candace, check there aren't any hostile curses on the body. And put that book somewhere safe."

"The room *was* safe," said Aunt Candace, but she pulled out her Biblio-Witch Inventory.

Xavier, meanwhile, stepped around the body and returned to my side. "I'll have to tell my boss another soul has vanished."

"Sure." I walked with him to the door. "I'll tell you if we figure anything out."

There was nobody else within sight, and that wailing alarm ought to have brought everyone in the library running downstairs. That suggested the killer had slipped in and out without being seen—or the cursed object was already in here. But why kill Tad? Had he just been in the wrong place at the wrong time, or was there another reason? Maybe the killer was trying to stop anyone else from getting their hands on that book. Which would be a valid motive, except that they'd had ample opportunity to do so over the last week. Nobody could watch every corner of the library at the same time.

I needed a warm mug of tea to soothe my nerves. Since nobody had given me instructions, I made for the kitchen. As I did so, Jet flew down to land on my shoulder. I didn't even jump this time.

"Did you see who killed him?" I asked.

The bird shook his head. *I guess he does understand me.* He took flight and swooped around to the stairs, hovering above the lowest step.

"You want me to go upstairs?"

He flapped his wings. Giving the stairs a warning look not to vanish or move, I walked quickly up to my room. The door lay open, and my heart sank. *What's gone missing this time?*

Nothing was missing. Instead, Dad's journal lay on my bed, as though it'd never been gone. Next to it sat Sylvester, a self-important look on his face.

"I knew it!" I said. "You stole it for Cass, didn't you?"

"The ingratitude!" he said. "I retrieved this from the reference section."

"What was it doing in there?" I said. *Oops.* That's what I got for speaking without thinking first.

"Not much, by the look of things," he said. "Certainly not making *insulting* accusations." He gave a sniff.

"All right, I made a mistake," I said. "Sorry. Someone just died downstairs and I'm a little on edge. Not to mention there's a group of murderous vampires after it."

"I am very much aware of that threat," he said. "That's why I endeavoured to help you, and you repay me by insulting me."

He took flight, nearly clipping the top of my head with a claw. I ducked and grabbed the journal, hugging it to my chest.

"I forgot I challenged him to find it," I told Jet. "I… may have suggested you'd find it before he did. Is he bothering you?"

The crow made a chirping noise that presumably meant no. Hmm. The owl might not have taken the journal, but I didn't entirely trust him.

I sat down on the bed and opened the journal. The text remained unreadable. I'd figured Dad had created the code himself, but perhaps it was magic-related instead. Though the biblio-witchery I'd seen so far had been written in English, and my aunts hadn't recognised the language. I turned the pages, finding it exactly as I remembered. Maybe I'd been too quick to judge Cass after all. I was sure I'd seen her carrying it, but there were probably a lot of small square books in here. *Well done, Rory.* I crossed my fingers that Sylvester wouldn't tell Cass what I'd said.

"Rory?" Estelle pushed open my door. "Are you okay?"

"I have Dad's journal." I held it up. "Sylvester found it in the reference section."

Her eyes brightened. "Oh, that's great! I'm glad to hear it. The police are downstairs, and I worried they'd taken you away or something."

"I found the body, but it's obvious I didn't do it. The problem is, it doesn't look like the book of curses did, either."

Someone had slipped in and out and killed Tad without being detected. Like a ghost. Or a vampire. But vampires couldn't cast curses. Right?

Unsurprisingly, the atmosphere at dinner that evening was subdued, even when Cass graced us with her presence. She was so non-talkative that I honestly couldn't tell whether the owl had told tales on me or not. Aunt Candace, on the other hand, seemed unusually cheerful, chatting nonstop while we ate.

"So you found the missing journal," she said, when we were finishing off our meals.

I reached into my bag. "Sylvester found it for me. In the reference section."

Cass looked quickly in my direction then looked away again. I couldn't read her expression, but I was sure she looked a little startled for a second. "Seriously?" she said. "The owl never does anything for free."

"I told him that Jet would find it first, so he took it as a challenge." I put the book down on the table.

Aunt Candace leaned over eagerly. "Let's see what Roger wanted to hide."

"Nobody can read it," I said. "Even Aunt Adelaide couldn't."

"Maybe it was closed off to you before because you weren't magical," Aunt Candace said in thoughtful tones.

"Why the sudden interest?" Cass asked.

Aunt Candace shrugged. "Dealing with that curse book reminded me I haven't had a pet project in a while. I'm wondering what Roger wanted to keep hidden from his family."

"Only if Rory agrees," Aunt Adelaide said. "Yes, it *is* curious, but don't forget those vampires are hunting down the book."

"That means it's valuable," said Aunt Candace. "And packed with secrets."

Her pen and notebook floated under the table, scribbling away.

Aunt Adelaide sighed. "Yes, fine, we can have a look at it again. If that's okay with Rory."

"Sure," I said, pushing the journal to my aunts' side of the table. "The library keeps trying to shelve it. Twice it's gone missing and shown up on a random shelf."

"That so?" Aunt Candace all but snatched up the journal. "I'd need to run a few tests." She pulled out her Biblio-Witch Inventory, and my hands clenched under the table. After she'd blown her own eyebrows off trying to get that book of curses open, I wasn't sure I trusted her to handle it carefully.

"I don't know about this…" I reached for the journal, but Aunt Candace held it in the air.

Aunt Adelaide pointed her wand at the journal and levitated it back to my side of the table. "Candace, control yourself. This isn't a rare artefact we're dealing with, it's something very personal to Rory."

"Thanks." I took the journal again. "I found it in the back room of the bookshop and I assumed Dad wanted me to have it. Abe was the only other person there, and he was a normal."

"I'm aware of that," said Aunt Candace, looking aggrieved. "I only wanted a look."

"Or to snoop into Roger's life," Aunt Adelaide said. "Which is pointless, as that book isn't magical at all. If it was, the library would have alerted me."

"I didn't know that," I admitted. "I didn't know the vampires would follow me here, either."

"Don't blame yourself for that," Estelle said, drowning out Cass's derisive cough. "If it's not magical, maybe they want it for some other reason."

"I'd need a closer look to be sure," Aunt Adelaide said. "If that's okay with you, Rory."

"Sure." I passed her the journal, ignoring Aunt Candace's scowl. "Does the writing look familiar at all? I'm sure you've probably handled books written in dozens of languages in the library."

"We have," she confirmed. "This... no, I don't recognise it. If the library tried to shelve it in the reference section, that suggests it contains information. Vampires trade in knowledge. Maybe that's why they want it."

Aunt Candace turned to me, her pen still scribbling away. "She's right. Are you certain there wasn't a code-breaker document in the shop?"

"I never found it," I said. "And if there was, wouldn't the vampires have wanted that, too? Unless..."

Unless they could already read it? That couldn't be possible, not if Dad had made it so that even I couldn't understand it.

Aunt Adelaide shook her head. "Not if it contains information on the magical world. He wouldn't have put it in a place where a normal could get their hands on it."

"But what could possibly be that important?" I asked. "I mean, he left the magical world behind. He didn't know anything about the library that you don't already, right?"

Cass made a sceptical noise, and I glanced in her direction.

"What?" I said.

She shrugged. "If I were you, I'd have asked more questions when I had the chance."

"What, to Dad? He never gave away he was paranormal even for a second," I said. "I couldn't have known to ask if I didn't know this world existed, could I?"

"Exactly," she said. "You didn't know. Anything."

Estelle rose from her seat. "Cass, that's enough. You've done nothing but try to make Rory feel unwelcome since she arrived."

"You only just noticed?" Cass shot back at her, bounding to her feet. "I'm done with this nonsense."

She turned on the spot and stormed out of the room.

I shook my head. "Why would she be so insulted that I didn't ask Dad what the book was for? I didn't even know it existed until after he died."

Aunt Adelaide looked up from the journal. "Cass is displeased by the threat to the library. Since we can't understand the text in the journal, we can only speculate about what the vampires want it for. And as long as it remains in the library, it puts all of us at risk."

Oh. Cass didn't want *me* here, but if I left with the journal and lost it to the vampires, the library's secrets might be compromised, assuming that's what Dad had written about. No wonder she was so annoyed at me. Didn't make it my fault, though.

Aunt Adelaide handed me the journal back. "If the library keeps trying to shelve it, I'd carry it with you from now on. Or you could leave it in one of our secure rooms."

"Ah—I think I'll carry it instead." I tucked the journal under my arm. "Thanks."

"C'mon," said Estelle. "I'll make tea, and we can watch a film. I haven't shown you my room yet."

"You have a TV in here?"

"Of course. We don't live in the Stone Age." She grinned. "Just tell me what you like."

"I'm about five years behind. Dad never had a television and I didn't have the money."

"No worries, we'll find something."

Aunt Candace looked disappointed when I put the journal back in my bag, but she didn't try to take it again, and Estelle and I left the dining room. I expected the stairs to mess with me on the way up, but the library seemed to be on its best behaviour tonight.

"So," Estelle said. "How did your walk with the Reaper go?"

"It wasn't really a walk," I said. "I mean, we went to see the curse-breaker. I couldn't go alone, since you know, there's a vampire chasing me."

"Ah, yeah, vampires aren't fans of pointy objects. Except the obvious, that is." She bounded ahead to her room. "So what did Mr Bennet say? Was he as bad as last time?"

"Worse," I said. "Well, he did confirm Dominic was the one he borrowed the curse book to help, but he claimed it was to do with fang-shrinking curses or something. But that's the second time his name's come up in connection to this case."

Estelle paused with her hand on the doorknob to her room. "Dominic wasn't in when Tad died, though. You think he did it?"

"I don't know what to think," I admitted. "I'd blame the book of curses, but Aunt Candace picked it up and she was fine, and Xavier would know if it had anyone's soul trapped in it. He said."

"Xavier did, did he?" She gave a wry smile. "You two talked a lot? I don't think I've ever seen him take an interest in anyone before."

I frowned. "Really? He seems pretty outgoing."

She pushed the door open, revealing a room the same size as mine but much more cluttered. A huge TV occupied one wall. "The problem is his boss," she said. "The Grim Reaper has a reputation. I sometimes see him in the library, but he keeps to himself. Shame, given how smoking *hot* he is. Don't deny it—you noticed."

"I did notice," I admitted. "But I guess being a Reaper is an important job, and now there are two souls missing right here in the library."

"So he's going to be hanging around a lot? That might be good news for you." She winked. "All right—what do you want to watch?"

1 2

When I woke up the following morning, the first thing I did was check Dad's journal was still under my pillow. From now on, I was carrying it everywhere with me.

I made my way down to the kitchen without any library-related mishaps and found breakfast waiting on the sideboard. Estelle waved me into the living room. "My mum left out some of that extra-strength coffee."

"Oh, awesome." I picked up my plate and mug and joined her on the sofa. "It's Monday morning and the stairs didn't collapse on me. Did I wander into another library overnight?"

There was a sniff from the back of the sofa. Sylvester gave me a dirty look. I smiled placatingly, but he took off in a flutter of wings.

"Uh-oh," said Estelle. "What did you say to him?"

"I accidentally accused him of stealing the journal yesterday." I took a bite of toast, which was flavoured with raspberry jam today. "Since I found him in my room with the journal after we found Tad's body."

She winced. "That explains why he's in such a mood. In fairness, it's the sort of thing he'd do as a joke. But he's the one who found the journal?"

"Only because I said Jet would find it first."

She sipped her coffee. "That's probably the best way to deal with him until he gets used to you. Appeal to his ego."

"Would the same work for Cass?"

"She's slow to accept change. Give it time."

We munched companionably for a bit. "Is the library open as usual today?"

"Of course," she said. "Mondays are one of our busiest days. We have the poetry night, which is always a laugh."

"I think I'll sit that one out." The memory of Tad's death was too raw. Not to mention Duncan's.

"Oh, Rory," said Aunt Adelaide, entering the room. "Good, you're here. Aunt Candace wanted me to give you this."

I took the magical theory textbook she offered me. "Do I have another magic lesson, then?"

"Tomorrow," she said. "Your aunt's left details of the assignment inside. I know theory is dull work, but the quicker you pass your first exam, the quicker you'll get a wand."

"Oh, good," I said. "I'd feel much more secure if I had a way to defend myself against those vampires."

"You won't have to worry about that for long." She smiled and nodded to Estelle. "Take Rory to get her Biblio-Witch Inventory."

My heart jumped. "I get one of those? For real?"

Estelle grinned. "Told you so."

"In the meantime, you can start the theory exercise in your own time," Aunt Adelaide added, leaving the living room. "My sister will probably forget to check, but you'll need them for the exam."

"Don't bother with that now," Estelle said in an under-

153

tone. "Really, you want that book. It'll be up on the third floor."

I was almost as buoyant as Estelle as I followed her through the library, up a spiralling staircase to the third level.

Estelle pulled a key out of her pocket and approached one of the locked doors marked with an X.

"Why does the door need a padlock on it?" I asked.

"Words can be slippery," she said. "You never know when they're going to escape. Close the door behind you and watch your back."

That sounded ominous.

She unlocked the door, then pulled out her Biblio-Witch Inventory and tapped the page once. The door sprang open.

A single book lay on the table inside, its cover black with no writing on it. I approached and picked it up, half-expecting it to light up or something dramatic. Instead, all the pages were blank.

"It'll fill up when you start learning magic," Estelle said. "In the meantime..." She passed me a notebook and pen, both of which were marked with the family's coat of arms.

My hand closed around the pen, a smile blooming. *Finally.* I had all my real biblio-witch gear. That proved I belonged here, right? "So I write the words in the book as I learn them?"

She nodded. "When you learn a new word, make sure you write it in the Biblio-Witch Inventory so you can use it any time. Or just use the pen and notebook if you're in a hurry. You can also still write on any available paper, since the power comes from you, not just the tools, but they help."

The door slammed open behind us and Cass bellowed, "We need you downstairs. Now."

I looked at Estelle in alarm. "Not another murder?"

"I hope not."

I put the Biblio-Witch Inventory, pen and notebook into

my bag and followed her out of the room, which locked itself behind us.

Beyond the foot of the spiral stairs, a large pile of boxes stood beside the front desk.

"New delivery," Cass said. "We have to get these to the right sections before the clients get their paws on—stop that," she snapped at Samson, the persistent late-returner, who'd tried to remove a book from the pile. He had some nerve, considering Cass was in an even fouler mood than usual, by the look of things.

"A delivery? That's all?" I said. "I thought someone died."

She rolled her eyes. "So dramatic."

"Someone *did* die," Estelle said. "Fine, Rory and I will help out if you don't disappear after two minutes like you usually do."

Cass merely glared at me and picked up a book. I'd bet she'd interrupted my biblio-witch induction on purpose, but someone needed to keep an eye on Samson and other potential thieves. We sorted books into piles while Aunt Adelaide staffed the front desk. Several people asked after Tad and offered their condolences on his death, but none seemed to be put off coming into the library. Apparently, the risk of death at the hands of a paperback was an occupational hazard.

I sorted book after book. One of them was bound in heavy chains. Another blew out puffs of smoke whenever anyone touched it. Aunt Adelaide took care of the 'dangerous' section, which left Estelle and me to split the rest with Cass.

To no surprise, Cass disappeared halfway through. I picked up the book she'd abandoned, a law volume, and made my way to the Reading Corner to return it to the shelf. At least I knew my way around that part of the library.

I checked the number again and found the right spot on

the shelf. When I put the book into place, it stayed where it was. The shelf didn't start moving, the floor didn't give way, and the laws of physics remained in place. Sorted. I walked back around the shelves to avoid directly passing the hammock where Tad used to lie and walked headlong into Dominic coming the other way.

"My apologies," he said smoothly. "I didn't see you there."

I backed up a step. "I thought you could read my mind."

"I was lost in my own thoughts. As I'm sure you were, too." He flashed me a smile. With fangs. It hit me in a rush that I was alone behind a long row of bookshelves with a vampire. Cold sweat gathered on my forehead and my body tensed.

"Don't let me keep you." He took off at a brisk walk and was gone.

I breathed out, walking past the corridor he'd been blocking. That was the way into our family's living quarters. What was he doing there?

I halted. There was something on the floor beside the stairs that led up to my room. It looked like... red sand.

The same type of sand the vampires had used to set me on fire.

I ran all the way to the front desk. "Aunt Adelaide," I called.

She jumped up from the desk and ran towards me, her hair flying behind her.

"What is it?" she asked. "Goddess, not another one?"

"No, but there's something—look." I led the way to the corridor leading to our living quarters and showed her the glowing sand on the floor. "I recognise it—it's what the vampire used to burn down the bookshop. Or tried to."

She knelt down to look. "Oh, that's firedust. We have some in our store cupboard. Maybe Candace or Cass needed to use it and accidentally dropped some on the way out."

Maybe, but the firedust was right next to the stairs leading up to my room. Had the vampire been up there? The downside to having so many patrons wandering in and out was that nowhere was off limits, not if the library didn't want it to be. But if Dominic had wanted the journal, then he could have taken it from me when we'd collided and nobody would ever have caught him.

Aunt Adelaide scooped the firedust into her hand and entered the kitchen. A cupboard door lay half-open, showing shelves containing various ingredients in bottles. Sure enough, there was an open bag labelled 'Firedust' peeking out. She carefully tipped the firedust from her hand into the bag. "Candace probably wanted to burn a manuscript that wasn't working. Wouldn't be the first time."

"I ran into that vampire again," I blurted. "Dominic, I mean. Just there. I didn't think patrons could walk this close to our living quarters."

He hadn't hurt me, either, though he'd had ample opportunity when we'd been alone together. But what about the firedust? Even if it got there by accident, it was a downright dangerous substance to spill in a library.

"Is that so?" Aunt Adelaide closed the cupboard door. "He's a regular visitor. I can go and find him, if it worries you."

I shook my head. "He's probably disappeared by now. I guess I'm just jumpy."

My aunt briefly rested her hand on my arm. "I understand, Rory, believe me. But you're safe here."

I gave a small nod. She left the kitchen and I followed close behind, my gaze darting to the spot where the firedust had lain. The carpet was clear, but on the stairs, a thin trickle of sand marked the lower steps.

I crouched and picked it up, turning it over in my hands. Aunt Candace appeared, descending the stairs, muttering under her breath. I jumped out of the way before she walked into me.

"Oh, you're still here," she said distractedly.

"Why wouldn't I be?" I asked. "Er... Aunt Adelaide said you removed some of that firedust from the cupboards. Did you? Because I ran into Dominic—"

Her whole body went still. "If you tell anyone," she said, "I will write you a horrible death scene."

The firedust slipped from my hand. "Tell anyone what?"

A notebook and pen appeared at her side. I took a wary step back. Was she really threatening me? Why would she and the vampire conspire together?

"Aunt Candace... is Dominic one of the vampires after the journal?" I asked. "Did he kill Tad?"

"Excuse me?" Edwin's voice said loudly. The elf policeman approached us, looking at Aunt Candace, then me.

Aunt Candace's notebook disappeared into her pocket. "Oh, it's you," she said. "What are you doing here?"

"It looked like you were terrifying your niece," he observed. "What was that about vampires?"

Aunt Candace looked me over. "She seems fine to me. Nobody mentioned vampires."

"She just did," said Edwin. "I think you'd better come with me."

My aunt folded her arms. "I don't think so."

"Are you threatening an officer of the law?"

Aunt Candace made an exasperated noise. "No, I'm not threatening anyone."

Two trolls appeared behind the elf, blocking the way into the library.

"Just what is going on?" Cass's voice rang out.

"Your aunt's being rude to the chief of police," Aunt Adelaide informed her. "Edwin, there must have been a misunderstanding."

"I understood perfectly clearly," he said, in cold tones. "I heard her making threats. Something about death."

"In a book!" Aunt Candace said. "And for your information, Dominic did nothing wrong."

"Is that so?" Edwin beckoned to her. "Come on, and we'll talk somewhere more appropriate."

Aunt Candace made an irritated noise, but the presence of the two hulking trolls encouraged her to follow the chief of police back into the library.

Cass gave me a glare. "What did you do?"

"Nothing," I said. "I ran into her on the stairs and she threatened to kill me off in one of her books if I told anyone something. The problem is I'm not sure what that something was."

Aunt Candace twisted to face me. "Wait, you don't? What did you say to Dominic?"

"I didn't," I said. "I ran into him here right when I saw that firedust on the floor. I thought the vampires were trying to burn the place down."

"The firedust?" Aunt Candace said. "No, I brought the dust out to destroy that blasted curse book. I've had bloody enough of it. I must have dropped some of it on the way."

"You can tell me all about it," Edwin said, and the trolls flanked Aunt Candace until she walked away. I heard her yelling from the library entrance, and Aunt Adelaide and Estelle hurried after her. Before I could join them, Cass barred my way.

"I can't believe your nerve," she hissed. "First you barge in here and disrupt all our lives, now you're getting us arrested."

"Okay, I made a mistake!" I said. "Look, there was dust all over the floor out here and I thought it might catch fire."

"Goddess, you're ridiculous," she said. "Firedust wouldn't work in this place. That vampire was talking complete nonsense. Look." She yanked out her Biblio-Witch Inventory and tapped a word. Flames sprang up on the floor, but the instant they appeared, a cloud of smoke descended, swallowing them up. "Library's defences. See?"

I gaped at the spot where the flames had vanished. "So the vampire—Mortimer Vale—was just bluffing? He didn't know?"

"You're still telling that story?"

I blinked. "You don't believe me?"

She snorted. "Sure. It's too convenient. You happened to get yourself threatened by vampires right when your magic showed up, so you decided to barge into our lives as though we weren't all doing perfectly fine without an extra person to train. The library is ours."

"I don't see why there shouldn't be room for someone else," I said. "I'm sorry about your aunt, but I'm here now, and I'm not going anywhere."

"Sure, you *say* that," she said. "You didn't see what the library was like after your dad left. It was a wreck for weeks. We couldn't walk down corridors without it raining frogs."

Really? If she was telling the truth, Dad had left for my sake. She must know that. "Were you the one setting the library against me? To drive me off before it got too attached?"

Her mouth twitched. "So what if I was? You don't belong here. And if it's true that those vampires are after that journal of yours, then you're a danger to all of us and you should leave. Unless you want to give *me* the journal instead and save us all the hassle."

"Was it you who took it from my room?" It was about time we cleared the whole thing up.

"Not directly." She scowled. "The library tried to shelve it. If it contains our secrets, it belongs in the library. You don't."

She about-turned and left me standing there in the corridor, unable to rid myself of the sinking feeling that I'd just wrecked my new life before it'd even got off the ground.

A soft caw caught my attention. Jet. I held out my hand and let him land on it. My familiar. *He* wanted me to stay. I just had to hope I hadn't completely messed things up.

E stelle found me sitting morosely at the study desk in one of the classrooms. Was there even any point in doing my theory work exercises if my aunt was going to jail?

"Hey," she said. "Sorry about earlier."

"Me, too. I can't believe I got Aunt Candace arrested."

"She didn't exactly make an effort to defend herself," she said. "I'd almost think she wanted to get arrested."

"What, for research? Like the dust?" I laid my head down on the table. "I should have just asked if it was actually possible to burn the library down before I lost my head over that vampire."

Her brow wrinkled. "You couldn't have known. The police will get to the truth and she'll be back before we know it."

"And if not? Cass hates me, too. She admitted she's the one who's been setting the library against me."

Estelle put a comforting arm around me. "Don't let her intimidate you. Give it time, she'll come around to the idea of having another witch around."

"She said it's because my dad left and upset the library," I said. "I didn't know she'd remember."

"Ah," said Estelle. "I'm guessing she meant... I'll have to ask my mum, but she said your dad did come to visit once or twice when you were a baby but wasn't able to stay. For obvious reasons. I guess it upset the library that he was gone."

"Yeah." I sighed. "Anyway, she's angry with me for getting Aunt Candace arrested now. And Dominic, if they found him."

"He's at the police station, as far as I heard. Not sure if they arrested him or not, but he's vehemently denying he killed either of the victims."

"I don't think he's the killer." I'd even messed *that* up. But what had I missed? I'd been so sure the vampires were involved.

"That's in the police's hands now," Estelle said. "As for us, we have to get the place ready for the poetry night."

"The... hang on," I said, lifting my head. "Poetry night? Is the poetry night held in the Reading Corner?"

"Unless the others want to move it elsewhere. It'll be weird without Tad watching from the hammock."

The hammock. I hadn't thought to look over there to see if Tad had left any clues behind. Call it intuition or just grasping at straws, but there must be some reason he'd been targeted.

Had he witnessed the first death? Was that why they'd killed him?

We left the classroom for the empty Reading Corner, where I made straight for the hammock where Tad used to lie. It was untouched, and inside it was the pointy hat he'd been wearing the last time I'd seen him.

I picked it up and a piece of paper fell out, covered in

scribbled lines. Poetry. The first line read, 'Let the nefarious rites begin'. That sounded familiar.

"Estelle?" I said. "What happened to that slip of paper that was in the cursed book?"

"What about it?" Estelle asked.

"This is the same poem." I held up the paper. "Did Tad get it out of the book?"

"No, he couldn't have done," she said. "From the way he was lying, he died the instant he touched the book."

I examined the scrap of paper. It sure looked similar to what I remembered of the poem we'd found in the book of curses. "But that means the other piece of paper is missing. The one from the book. Did he have it on him when they removed the body?"

"Duncan's poetry?" She frowned. "Why would Tad have a copy?"

"Maybe he was a fan," I said, but my mind was racing. "It was the last thing Duncan wrote before he died. Maybe it counts as evidence."

"Let's check the book again," she said, walking across the Reading Corner. "Pretty sure Aunt Candace just left it there in the room."

"She said she was going to burn it, though."

"My mum would kill her if she did."

This time, the door to the spare room was locked. One tap from Estelle's wand opened it. The book of curses wasn't floating in a circle this time but lay on a table in the room's centre, unmarked.

I approached it apprehensively, then picked up the book. The cover felt leathery, the pages were yellowed, and I didn't drop dead. Good start.

Taking in a breath, I opened the book at random, then I held it up to let the pages spread. No scraps of paper fell out.

Estelle frowned. "I should have asked Edwin if he found

any bits of paper on Tad's body. I wouldn't have thought to look. Is the poem exactly the same?"

I held up the crumpled paper again. "Yes, but I think the handwriting is different. Maybe Tad copied it out if he was a fan."

"I thought he couldn't write," said Estelle.

I looked down at the page again. It didn't contain any clues on its own, just a string of dubiously connected lines. But I was sure it must be evidence. It wouldn't endear me any more to the police if I showed up so soon after they'd hauled off my aunt, but guilt at Aunt Candace's imprisonment would gnaw away at me until I did something about it.

"Late customer," Estelle said, at the sound of the doorbell. "I'll get Mum, you ask what he wants, okay?"

"Sure." I left the room, pocketing the scrap of paper. Evidence or not, I still needed to do my job.

I crossed the library to the front desk—and froze.

Mortimer Vale smiled back at me. "Those are some very clever wards you have on this library," he said. "Very clever. Now, give me the journal."

"I won't."

His teeth flashed, and his body blurred as he vaulted the counter. I dove to the floor, my hand in my bag and grasping for the pen and notebook. He landed beside me, reaching out, but I'd already pressed pen to paper. *Fly.*

The books stacked on the desk rose into the air, knocking the vampire off his feet. He was upright in a heartbeat, but they flew at him again, forcing him to move around the desk towards the doors.

"You can't keep me out forever, Aurora," he said. "I *will* have that journal."

He disappeared, the merest rattle of the doors betraying that he'd been there at all.

I released a breath, my hands shaking. The books which

had chased him dropped to the floor and I quickly moved to retrieve them.

As I did so, Aunt Adelaide appeared. "Rory? Who was it?"

"The vampire," I said. "Mortimer Vale. He got past the wards on the library. I threw the books at him, but he escaped."

Aunt Adelaide swore. "Right. I was already on my way to the police station. We'll both go this time."

"The poetry night, though?"

"Estelle can take over," she said, returning the books to the desk with a flick of her wand. "We'll go now before it gets dark."

I didn't like the idea of carrying the journal on me with Mortimer Vale so close, but it was that or leave it behind. "How did he break the wards?"

"He didn't break them." She swept towards the doors and outside into the chilly evening air. Her Biblio-Witch Inventory was in her hand, and she looked the building up and down. "If he found a gap in the wards, there's only one person outside the library who might have told him."

"Who?"

She turned away from the library and broke into a fast stride across the square. "The curse-breaker."

"The—wait, what?" I ran after her. She was way fitter than I was. Probably from charging around the library all the time. "How would he know?"

"Because there was a time when my sister and I wanted to break the curse on the library," she said. "He's the only person we told."

I frowned at her. "But I thought he hated the library."

"He hated dealing with its magic," she said. "In the end, he was unable to undo any of the spells your grandmother put on the library, and we're glad of it."

We reached the seafront and she directed her pace

towards the decrepit little shop. I'd have picked anyone else to ask for help, but I trusted Aunt Adelaide's judgement more than mine at the moment.

Mr Bennet looked about as thrilled to see me as I was to see him. "You again?"

Aunt Adelaide approached his desk. "We're here to ask if you gave anyone a consultation on breaking wards this week," she said. "Someone tried to get into the library."

"Customer confident—"

"These men want my niece dead," said Aunt Adelaide, in dangerous tones. "I'd advise you to think carefully before refusing to answer me."

He took a step backwards. "I heard they arrested your sister. I could report you for threatening me, too."

"Oh, this isn't a threat," said Aunt Adelaide. "There's a hostile vampire in town intending harm to my family, and he slipped past the wards on the library. I know you kept that research."

His jaw set. "I sell to anyone who buys from me. I don't give away information for free. I told nobody how to break your wards."

"If I find you're lying, then I'll have to report you," she said.

"Naturally." His tone was sour. "If I could curse that abomination of a library out of existence, I would."

Delightful.

"He's not guilty," she muttered to me on the way out. "Unfortunately. I'd love to see those trolls cart him away."

She led us to a square building facing the pier. The local police station was smaller than I'd expected, though everywhere seemed that way after the library. Inside, Edwin stood in conversation with another elf beside a desk at the front.

"Adelaide, I have spent entirely too much time dealing with your family," he said. "No, you may *not* see your sister."

Aunt Candace's voice drifted through an open door. "I'm being deprived!"

"She's being incredibly uncooperative," he said. "Keeps demanding access to her manuscript."

"Ignore her," said Aunt Adelaide. "I came here to report a break-in. The rogue vampire got *into* the library and threatened my niece. He fled when cornered."

The chief of police turned to Aunt Adelaide with a long-suffering expression. "I'll send someone over to your property shortly if you'd like to wait in here."

Aunt Adelaide huffed. "There's a public event happening in the library right now. We can't have people breaking in and threatening our patrons."

Aunt Candace shouted something unintelligible.

"I already arrested one vampire today," said Edwin. "I don't know what else you expect me to do."

"Wait, you *did* arrest Dominic?" I said. "I thought—but he's not the vampire who came after me."

His gaze snapped onto me. "You mean to say he had no connection with the case?"

"Not this Mortimer Vale person," said my aunt. "The vampires who followed Rory here are strangers from outside town."

Edwin scowled. "You might have mentioned that before. I was under the impression you were still looking at that blasted cursed book."

"Actually," I said, "I wanted to ask you a question. It's about Duncan's poetry."

"What about it?" Edwin shot a disgruntled look in the direction of Aunt Candace's continued shouts.

"I found this where Tad used to sit in the library, before he died." I pulled the scrap of paper from my pocket. "Why would he have kept one of Duncan's poems? It's not written in his handwriting, either."

"Oh, the eccentric normal?" he asked. "It's a shame, but I don't think any piece of writing from him counts as reliable evidence."

"It's not his, though," I said. "Duncan wrote it. The original paper disappeared. Was Tad holding a piece of paper when you brought him in?"

"No." He winced at another shout from Aunt Candace. "Really, now. I'll go and see what she wants."

He disappeared through a side door, followed by the other elf.

"I was sure it was connected," I said to Aunt Adelaide. "Tad… I swear he said something that sounded like a line of poetry once or twice."

Including when we'd found Duncan's body.

Aunt Adelaide grimaced as her sister's raised voice came through the door. "Candace had better behave herself at the trial. Edwin is fair, but she's not helping her own case."

"No," I said. "But what I'd like to know is—how did the vampire get past the wards? Does that mean anyone can get in? Even… even right now?"

Aunt Adelaide stiffened. "In theory—yes. I think we'd better head back to the library."

"The poetry night is just opening," Aunt Adelaide said breathlessly, slowing down to open the library doors.

Sure enough, the ground floor had filled with people—witches, wizards, satyrs, nymphs, but no vampires. Or Aunt Candace. Another pang of guilt shook me. "Would Aunt Candace be bothered about missing this?"

"Oh, no," said Aunt Adelaide. "She *hates* reading her work out in public. She's never taken part in one of the poetry nights before."

She'd probably never spent the night in a cell before either. "Is there anyone here who shouldn't be?"

"I'll keep a close watch on everyone in the room," she said firmly. "Sylvester?"

"At your service," said the owl, flying down to land on the front desk. "What can I do for you?"

"I want you to tell me if anyone leaves the Reading Corner," Aunt Adelaide said.

"Wouldn't watching the door be more logical?" he enquired. "I might have eyes in the back of my head on occasion, but I can't be in two places at once."

"Then I'll ask Jet," I said. "Hey, Jet."

Sylvester ruffled his feathers. "Actually, if I find a certain spot in the Reading Corner, I'll be able to see the door. I have excellent eyesight."

Jet flew over and landed on my shoulder. Sylvester's owl-eyes followed the movement, and he huffed. "Involving the crow isn't necessary. He can't even talk."

"Jet, can you watch the door and warn us if anyone comes in?" I asked the crow. "Don't look at me like that, Sylvester. I'm trying to stop evil vampires from breaking into the library and murdering everyone. The more people I have watching out for trouble, the better."

Jet cawed in agreement. He and the owl had a kind of stare-off, then Sylvester spread his wings. "I'm far more intimidating than he is."

Appeal to the ego. "Right, you are," I said. "That means if the killer is hiding somewhere in the library right now, you'll be the first to chase them off, right?"

The owl drew himself up with a self-important air. "Obviously."

"Is the poetry night starting anytime soon?" said an irritable voice behind me. Samson, or Late Fee Guy. "The host has vanished."

"Oh, Estelle," said Aunt Adelaide. "I don't know where she —I'll find her. Rory, go to the Reading Corner."

Jet cawed. "Go on," I said to him. "If you see anything, you'll warn me, okay?"

He made a noise of assent, then took flight to guard the door. Despite our two guards, I wished we'd brought the police here. Still, at least I'd have warning if the vampire tried to sneak in again.

On my way to the Reading Corner, I checked my biblio-witch notebook and pen were within easy reach in my pocket, and a slip of paper fell out. Duncan's poem. I'd forgotten I was carrying it.

"What's that?" Samson asked.

"Nothing." I pocketed it again. "I didn't know you took part in poetry nights." Lucky there didn't seem to be any sign of Cass around. Was this why he still kept hanging around the library despite his habit of returning books late?

I made for the Reading Corner and found a free bean bag. When I moved it, a book fell out from underneath it, a small square one. I couldn't be sure, but it looked like the one Cass had been reading before. I opened it and spotted a familiar title. It was one of Aunt Candace's paperbacks, and inside it was Cass's name. I read the first paragraph, hiding a grin. Cass was secretly a fan, despite her projected disdain for her aunt's books. Judging by the first paragraph, it was very well-written. If all the poets turned out to be terrible, then at least I'd have something else to read.

A hush fell over the library, indicating the opening of the poetry night. The candles came on, making the open space look like a stage.

"Before we begin," Estelle said, "I thought we should pay our respects to a member we recently lost..."

A faint disparaging noise came from my right. Late Fee Guy had sat next to me and gave me an ugly look when he saw the paperback in my hands. *Who cares what he thinks*

The first poet took to the stage, a satyr with long red hair. His poem was an ode to an ex-girlfriend and went on for seventeen pages. Four people fell asleep, and when Samson started snoring, the satyr paused. "Part Two, coming next week," he finished.

Several people groaned.

Next up was a group of elves, who recited an equally long poem in a language nobody could understand. I resumed reading Aunt Candace's book instead and only tuned in again when Samson stood up beside me, swaggering to the stage. He cleared his throat loudly, to wake the sleeping audience members, then began his recital.

It was about as bad as I'd expected. I adjusted my position so he wouldn't be able to see me reading, turning the page of the book. Someone had written in the margins. I squinted at the lines, frowning. It looked like poetry. Samson had got into trouble for writing in the books once already. No wonder Cass had been mad at him, if it'd been *her* books he'd written in.

Hang on. I knew that handwriting. I'd seen it on the piece of paper I'd found in Tad's hammock. The paper with one of Duncan's poems written on it.

An uneasy flutter went through me. If I compared the handwriting to what I remembered of the other piece of paper from the cursed book, it wasn't the same, I was sure. Two people had written down the same poem. But who'd written it first? Tad had known the poem—he'd recited its first line at one point—but Estelle had been certain he couldn't write. He didn't even know his own name.

I leaned over to where Samson had been sitting and sneaked a glance at the book he'd left half-open beside his seat. I had to crane my neck to read it, but one glance confirmed the handwriting matched the note in my pocket.

Samson had copied Duncan's poem. Or the other way around. Was he trying to steal credit for his work after his death, or was there something else going on? One of them had copied the other—and only one of them was dead. But the only way to prove anything would be to find the other piece of paper. The one that had fallen from the book.

Samson finished reciting and looked expectantly at the audience as though hoping for applause. Some people clapped half-heartedly, but most were asleep or otherwise disengaged. I slipped out of my seat and shuffled around the shelves to where Estelle sat.

"Hey," I whispered. "I don't suppose you know where that paper went?"

She blinked. "What paper?"

"You know the book of curses? That piece of paper we found inside it, the one with poetry on it?."

"We already checked the room," she whispered back. "Why?"

"I thought Duncan wrote it, but I just saw Samson's handwriting and it matches the second copy of the poem I found. The one that was in Tad's hammock."

She frowned. "Really?"

Tad had known the words of the poem. He must have heard it before. I looked at the central stage and saw Samson had gone. Wait, wasn't Sylvester supposed to be keeping an eye on things?

"Where's that owl?"

Estelle looked up at the shelf where the owl had been sitting. "Good question. Sylvester?"

A couple of people looked up, but most remained half-asleep. I stepped backwards, my gaze searching the shelves for the owl—and the bookshelf behind me moved suddenly. I stumbled over my feet, into an unfamiliar corridor.

"Ah." Oh, no. I didn't recognise where I was. It was too dark. "Library, this really isn't the time."

"It wasn't the library." Samson stepped into the corridor before me. He held a piece of paper in his hands. "Were you looking for this, Aurora?"

15

"**D**id you write that?" I indicated the paper. "And Duncan copied you? Or was it the other way around?"

"I wrote every word," he spat. "Every word of it. He stole it from me."

The library was quiet, as though the books were holding their breaths. Worse, there was no sound from the Reading Corner at all, and I didn't recognise the corridor the library had brought me to.

He noticed me looking. "The library's actually pretty easy to fool, if you're adept with words. And I'm a master."

I suppressed a snort, despite myself. Those mangled lines he'd recited weren't the words of someone with a poetic mind.

"What's so funny?"

I shook my head. "It's just so absurd. You used your poem as a bookmark and wrote lines in every book you took out of the library. That's a careless thing to do if you're so concerned about being caught out for murder."

"I didn't leave it lying around out of carelessness." He gave the piece of the paper a shake, and I saw he was wearing gloves.

"The paper is cursed," I said. "That's what Duncan touched, not the book." And it was pure luck that nobody else had put their hands on it until Tad. After all, it'd been sealed inside the book before my aunt had cracked it open. "Why did you seal it?"

"I didn't. He did. He was trying to counter the curse, and it didn't work." He wasn't smiling. His mouth was a thin angry line. He was still mad at Duncan, even now.

"Look, I'm not saying stealing is a good thing, but murder? Why not report him over it?"

"I tried. The police didn't care." He scowled. "He said he put his heart and soul into those words, so I decided to take him literally."

"That's sick."

"So is stealing." He took a step forward. "He stole every word of mine and took credit for it. He had to be punished."

He was deranged. He was also blocking the way out. And *how* had he made the library move? Only biblio-witches were supposed to be able to do that.

"An innocent man died, too." My hand inched towards my pocket, but if that piece of paper of his came near me, I was dead.

"Tad? That's his problem. He was a freak anyway."

He heard you. He was trying to warn us. I took a step back. "I'm going to have to report you to the police."

"I can't let you do that." He was still holding the paper. "You're not the only one with the ability to manipulate words."

The page *moved,* jumping out of his hand and folding itself into a paper aeroplane. He gave a thin-lipped smile.

"That's my gift. I can manipulate paper. It took a while to learn how to do it on the wards, but there's nothing I can't learn from this library."

I backed up another step. He was the one we should have been keeping an eye on all along—and not because of the late returns issue. The vampire hadn't messed with the wards —*he* had.

The paper flew at me, warping into the shape of a bird. I dove behind the shelf, hoping the library would spring to my defence. I didn't know enough biblio-witch magic to stop him, let alone block a curse that had captured two people's souls.

"Hey! Sylvester!" I shouted. "Jet!"

"Do you really think I've made it possible for anyone to find us in here?" The paper bird flew at me again. I lunged for the nearest gap between the shelves, rolling out into another corridor. The place was a maze with no visible path back to familiar territory. Like he'd planned it.

I swallowed hard, holding myself behind the shelf. If he came around the corner, he'd see me. There were no floating lanterns in this dark corridor, but he wielded a curse and I was barely a witch.

"If you're thinking of using any of your new tricks, Aurora, you're wasting your time," he said. "Your magic isn't anywhere near enough to stand up to a curse."

No kidding. I doubted a beginner's spell would work on a deadly soul-trapping curse. I had to think of something. I dug in my pocket and pulled out the paper and pen, but no words came. *Think. Come on, think.*

The scrap of paper with Samson's poem on it fell from my pocket. The real, not the fake. *The curse isn't in the paper. It's in the words.* He'd written them, but he'd chosen to put the curse on the poem copied by Duncan.

What if I changed the words? What would happen to the curse then?

Magic rushed to my fingertips as I pressed the nib of the biblio-witch pen to the page. Line by line, I scratched over the words. Erasing them. Replacing them.

Free the missing souls.

Undo the curse.

A strangled yell came from the other side of the shelf, followed by the sound of paper tearing. Hoping it was working, I added, *Let Samson be caged in his own words.*

Samson yelled again, louder. I risked a peek through the gap in the shelves and watched him struggling against a set of ropes that'd appeared from thin air. The ropes shifted, revealing they were made of words, an endless string of floating letters. *Whoa.*

As he flailed, he fell back into the shelf, causing paperbacks to topple free. I dug in my pocket again, found the rolled-up parchment, and hit the alarm.

A wailing noise struck up, and the bookshelves shifted jerkily as though pulled by invisible strings. Through the gap, Jet flew towards Samson and landed on him, pecking at his face. He screamed and covered his head with his hands.

"Jet!" I said. "How do I get out of here?"

The crow cawed, fluttering over to the shelves. They'd moved aside, revealing a path back to the Reading Corner.

Trusting him to watch Samson, I sprinted out into the middle of the poetry night. "I've caught Samson," I gasped. "Look. He's the murderer."

The spectators stared at me. One of them clapped uncertainly.

"That doesn't rhyme," someone said.

"I mean, literally." I pointed, giving a clear view of Samson tied up with his own words.

"What happened to him?" asked the first speaker.

There was a joke in there somewhere about eating one's words, but I settled for saying, "Someone fetch Aunt Adelaide."

16

Aunt Adelaide appeared in an instant. "Samson? It was him who damaged the wards?"

"He also killed Duncan and Tad," I said. "He cursed the scrap of paper with the poem written on it—that's somewhere back there, too. It was the paper he cursed, not the book. But I undid it."

Everyone gaped at me, while Aunt Adelaide strode up to the corridor where he lay tied up. "What did he do back here?"

"Messed with the library's magic. He said his magic lets him manipulate pages..."

"Not for long," she said firmly.

Sylvester flew over my head, grabbed a struggling Samson by the scruff of his neck, and dragged him into the spotlight. Meanwhile, I walked through and picked up the paper bird.

"This was cursed," I explained to Aunt Adelaide. "He forgot he left another copy of the same poem lying around. Look." I held up the second piece of paper, handing both of them to my aunt. "The poem was originally written by Samson. Duncan stole it from him."

"And that's why he killed him," Aunt Adelaide said. "I see."

"I think Tad witnessed the murder and was trying to warn me," I said. "Then he went looking for the book and got cursed, too. We're lucky nobody else touched it, especially Aunt Candace."

Aunt Candace. She'd be able to walk away free now.

"Yes, we are," Aunt Adelaide said. "Very lucky."

She snapped her fingers and Sylvester released the struggling, swearing young wizard. "Very unimaginative use of the English language, young man," she said to him.

Samson's face went purple.

I grinned. "Jet, will you go and fetch Edwin?"

Jet departed with a caw, while Estelle rushed to my side. "Cass will be furious she missed this."

"Where in the world is she?" Aunt Adelaide muttered. "The police—they won't need to use handcuffs. You did a spectacular job with the spell, Rory. Caught in his own words—how apt."

I felt my entire face catch fire. A couple of the poetry night crowd clapped, and I ducked my head. "Uh, should I fetch Cass?"

It was about time I found out what she'd really been doing when she sneaked off. Aside from reading Aunt Candace's books, that is.

"I saw her heading upstairs," Estelle said. "She'll have heard the alarm, for sure."

Right. Time to clear this up.

I walked up the spiralling staircase, my heart hammering in my chest, my body still trembling with adrenaline. I didn't know which floor Cass was on, but I could guess. The entire upper section was deserted, and when I reached the third floor, darkness surrounded me.

The vampire leapt out of the gloom, hands grabbing for my throat. I gasped, fighting for breath—and Cass hit him over the head with a hardback book.

The vampire collapsed onto his front with a thud.

I blinked at her, astonished. "You just—"

"Yes, I did," she said, lowering the book. "I thought I heard something up here that shouldn't be."

"Except me?" I climbed to my feet, one eye on the fallen vampire. Apparently, even a vampire couldn't stand up to a swift knock on the head.

"You're not about to accuse me of letting him in, are you?" Cass said.

"No, I'm not. I just caught the murderer and I know he let the wards down. But—what *are* you doing up here? Aside from avoiding the poetry night?"

Cass made an impatient noise. "I knew you'd come nosing around. Fine."

She pushed open the door to the Magical Creatures Division and led the way to one of the out-of-bounds rooms with the marked X on the door. Inside the room was a huge tank, and in the tank—

"What *is* that?"

The creature in the tank looked like a horse, but pure white with a long mane.

"He's a kelpie. I found him washed up on the beach, injured. Sylvester's been helping me take care of him—and your crow, too. I can't release him into the sea in this state. He'll get eaten alive. Kelpies are native to Scotland, so I've no idea how he got this far south."

I stared at the horse. Cass had a soft side after all. Who knew?

She cleared her throat, looking embarrassed. "Anyway, we'd better get that vampire downstairs before he wakes up."

She closed the door and waved her wand at the vampire,

whose body levitated into the air, floating down the staircase. We followed close behind, and Cass deposited the vampire in a heap on the floor in the lobby.

The vampire lunged to his feet, running for the doors—and ran smack into the Reaper. Xavier looked down at the vampire, his scythe in his hand.

"I wouldn't try to run," he said. "Are you the one who's been bothering Rory?"

"He is," I confirmed.

The vampire moved, and so did Xavier, the scythe blocking his path. "It works on undead, too, you know," Xavier said. "I felt two souls move on."

"Oh yeah, we caught the criminal." I grabbed for my notebook and pen. "What should I do to him? Tie him up?"

"Let me deal with him." Aunt Adelaide's pen scrawled on her notepad and the vampire collapsed again, unconscious. "He'll wake up in a cell. I'd rather lock him up in one of our top-secret rooms, but there are rules."

"It was the paper that was cursed," I explained to Xavier. "Not the book. I'll explain in a minute."

Behind him, the doors opened once again. Edwin strode in, looking even more frazzled than earlier. Jet sat on his shoulder.

"Your bird wouldn't stop pecking me until I left," he said accusingly. "You'd better not be wasting my time."

"We found the killer," Aunt Adelaide announced. "Our wayward vampire showed up here as well. Very much real, as you can see."

Xavier stepped to my side as the doors opened wider to allow two troll policemen to enter. "Are you all right, Rory? I should have come sooner."

"You didn't miss much at the poetry night, trust me," I said. "It's a shame it ended up like this. Samson was a terrible poet anyway. I guess they're going to set Aunt Candace free."

"They will," said Estelle, approaching us. "And they'll lock *him* up, for sure."

"Are you going to release my sister, then?" Aunt Adelaide asked Edwin.

"Yes, yes, you can take her back. Please. The vampire, too." He indicated one of his companions, a stocky wizard who'd entered the library behind the trolls.

The wizard took out a wand, waved it, and Aunt Candace and Dominic appeared before us. Both looked a little rumpled, but otherwise fine.

Dominic eyed the prone vampire. "Is that your trouble-maker? I recognise him."

"You do?" I asked. "Er, sorry for suspecting you. He's the reason why. Him, and a couple of his friends."

Dominic scowled. "Yes, I know him. I looked up his name, and they're part of a group of hunters of rare artefacts."

My stomach lurched. We'd only caught one of them. The other two were still out there. "You knew, then? You know what they're after?"

"Whatever it is, I'll make it clear they are *not* welcome here." His fangs gleamed in his mouth, and I suppressed the urge to back away.

"Why would you?" I couldn't help asking. "I got you locked in jail. Not to mention my aunt."

"Oh, I had the time of my life," Aunt Candace said. Her notebook and pen floated at her side. "I have to write it all down."

"She claimed she needed to see the inside of the torture chambers, for research purposes—there aren't any," Dominic added. "I rather think letting her go has added years to Edwin's life."

"We can't all be immortals," she said to him.

"But what were you doing in our quarters?" Aunt Adelaide asked the vampire.

"Your aunt and I are involved," he said matter-of-factly.

"You two?" Aunt Adelaide looked between him and Aunt Candace with an expression of disbelief. "Really?"

"Is it so strange?" asked Aunt Candace, defensiveness in her voice. "I would have preferred *not* to make a public spectacle, but apparently it's that sort of week."

"Well, I hope for all our sakes that you don't do anything to get arrested again," Aunt Adelaide said.

"Oh, I think I have enough material for now." She yanked her pen and notebook out of the air and turned to the inert body of Mortimer Vale. "So—what did I miss?"

Xavier moved to my side as Aunt Adelaide launched into an explanation. "Are you sure you're okay, Rory?"

"Never better," I said honestly. "Does that mean your boss will stop berating you now?"

"Yes," he said. "Provided I report in, anyway." He clearly wanted to say more, but not with everyone watching.

"I think Rory should win the prize for tonight," said one of the poetry club members.

There was a murmur of agreement. "Yes," someone shouted. "Rory!"

My face heated up again. Xavier chuckled behind me, then he was gone.

I had every confidence I'd see him again, soon. Hopefully not with a dead body in tow. Even the Reaper got days off sometimes, right?

———

I sat behind the desk, greeting each customer as they came in. After all the excitement of my first week, it was a relief to do something with little risk of falling through the floor. Even if the library had been on its best behaviour lately.

The doors opened, and Mr Bennet approached the desk.

"Oh, Aurora," he said, placing three books in front of me. "I wanted to return these, and to apologise for the way I spoke to you before."

I blinked. That, I hadn't expected. "No need," I said. "Er, did you guess the curse was on the paper?"

"Paper?"

"There was a slip of paper with a poem written on it inside the book," I explained. "Samson cursed the words on the page. That's why touching the book was fine."

"And where is the paper?" he asked.

"I don't know, my aunt threw it out. The curse is undone. It's harmless now."

"Shame," he commented. "I would have liked to study it. No matter. May I have a copy of *Beginner's Bindings*?"

"Sylvester?" I said to the owl, and he flew off to fetch the right book. He was being nicer to me than before, confirming my suspicion that he'd been provoking me on Cass's orders. I wouldn't say we were exactly friendly with one another now, but she'd warmed considerably since my discovery of her guest on the third floor. It helped that I no longer suspected her of wanting to get her hands on the journal.

Despite Mortimer Vale being jailed, nobody had found the other two vampires yet. I guessed they hadn't shown up in town—if they had, they'd have come with him to threaten me. But one thing was certain: there was no place safer for my dad's journal than the library.

The curse-breaker took the book from Sylvester. I watched him leave, wondering just what he'd seen in the library to make eternal enemies of my aunts. Considering he'd wanted to study the cursed paper, you'd think he and Aunt Candace would get along better. Luckily for all of us, Aunt Candace had found a new distraction in the form of a new manuscript about a cursed space artefact and seemed to have entirely forgotten our argument.

Of course, Dominic might be a part of it. I'd often seen him going in and out of the library. Thankfully, he'd forgiven us for his stint in prison.

Aunt Adelaide cleared her throat behind me. "Rory?" she said. "I found this upstairs, and I think our dad would want you to have it."

She handed me a photograph of Dad standing beside Aunt Candace and Aunt Adelaide. At the back was a woman with grey hair in the same wild style as Aunt Candace, and the same curvy figure as Aunt Adelaide. She must be Grandma.

"Just in case you had any doubts we're your family," she said.

A lump grew in my throat and I blinked unexpected tears from my eyes. "Thank you."

"Also, I think it's time you added your first word to your Biblio-Witch Inventory."

"Is it?" I dug into my bag and pulled out my book and the pen. "Which word?"

"Find," she said. "That way you won't get lost. Bound to come in useful, right?

Find. I liked that. I might have lost one life, but I'd found a new one. I'd found a family. And I'd finally found somewhere I belonged.

ABOUT THE AUTHOR

Elle Adams lives in the middle of England, where she spends most of her time reading an ever-growing mountain of books, planning her next adventure, or writing. Elle's books are humorous mysteries with a paranormal twist, packed with magical mayhem.

She also writes urban and contemporary fantasy novels as Emma L. Adams.

Find Elle on Facebook at https://www.facebook.com/pg/ElleAdamsAuthor/

Or sign up to her newsletter at: smarturl.it/ElleAdamsNewsletter